THE SEER

LINDA JOY SINGLETON lives in northern California. She has two grown children and a wonderfully supportive husband who loves to travel with her in search of unusual stories.

She is the author of more than thirty books, including the The Seer series, the Dead Girl series, and the Strange Encounters series (all from Llewellyn/Flux). She is also the author of the Regeneration, My Sister the Ghost, and Cheer Squad series. Visit her online at www.LindaJoySingleton.com.

Magician's Muse

LINDA JOY SINGLETON

flux™
Woodbury, Minnesota

First Edition

Cover design and wand illustration by Lisa Novak

Flux, an imprint of Llewellyn Worldwide Ltd.

This is a work of fiction. Names, characters, places, and incidents are either the product of the author's imagination or are used fictitiously, and any resemblance to actual persons, living or dead, business establishments, events, or locales is entirely coincidental.

Library of Congress Cataloging-in-Publication Data
Singleton, Linda Joy.
    Magician's Muse / Linda Joy Singleton.—1st ed.
        p. cm.—(The seer ; 6)
    Summary: Sabine's psychic abilities, sleuthing skills, and courage are pushed to a dangerous edge as she deals with the mysterious disappearance of her ex-boyfriend Josh, a new threat against her boyfriend Dominic, evil magicians—both living and dead—and a coldblooded murder.
    ISBN 978-0-7387-1957-3
    [1. Psychic ability—Fiction. 2. Missing persons—Fiction. 3. Murder—Fiction. 4. Mystery and detective stories.] I. Title.
PZ7.S6177Mag 2010
[Fic]—dc22

2010019113

Flux
Llewellyn Worldwide Ltd.
2143 Wooddale Drive
Woodbury, MN 55125-2989
www.fluxnow.com

Printed in the United States of America

Also by Linda Joy Singleton

The Seer #1, *Don't Die Dragonfly*
The Seer #2, *Last Dance*
The Seer #3, *Witch Ball*
The Seer #4, *Sword Play*
The Seer #5, *Fatal Charm*

The Dead Girl series

Dead Girl Walking
Dead Girl Dancing
Dead Girl in Love

The Goth Girl Mysteries

Buried

Thanks to my agent,
Jennifer Laughran

And my editors,
Brian Farrey and Sandy Sullivan

Also to writer-friend-sister,
Kate Emburg

All that may come to my knowledge in the exercise of my profession or in daily commerce with men, which ought not to be spread abroad, I will keep secret and will never reveal.

… a modern Magician's Oath

1

The phone was going to ring.

I knew this for a fact—the way you see dark clouds in the sky and know it's going to rain. Premonitions were no big deal to me. But the flash of fear that came with this sudden knowing was scary. Someone was going to call and I wouldn't like what they told me. It could change my life. Not in a good way.

My cell phone sat on my desk beside my keyboard.

Only a few feet away. But I didn't move from my bed, where I sat cross-legged in a festive jumble of wrapping paper, tape, and ribbons. Seconds ago I'd been humming to my holiday playlist while transforming gift-wrap into *art* with glitter, foil paper, and miniature golden angels. Now my holiday spirit was dead.

Usually my psychic vibes clued me in on who was calling and I often made a game of caller-guessing. I tried to guess now; closing my eyes to concentrate, I picked up a masculine vibe. Someone close to my age and to my heart. Immediately I thought of Dominic. Oh no, please, not him! Ever since I broke up with my last boyfriend, things had been made of awesome with Dominic. We talked endlessly about hopes, dreams, and our future together. But what if something bad had happened to him?

My cell phone rang.

I jumped, knocking a roll of wrapping paper onto the floor. Then I stiffened like a statue, cold and frozen inside, and couldn't bring myself to answer.

Finally by the fifth ring, I couldn't take it anymore. I grabbed the phone and flipped it open—stunned to read the Caller I.D.

Josh DeMarco. My ex-boyfriend.

But when I answered the call, it wasn't Josh. It was his mother.

"Sabine?" Mrs. DeMarco asked in an odd, anxious voice. "Are you there?"

"Yeah," I managed, through my surprise. My phone vibes usually weren't this far off.

"Sorry to call you so early," she told me.

"No problem. I'm an early riser." A million questions slammed into my head but I focused on the most important one. "Um ... how is Josh?"

"I—I don't know." She spoke so softly, her voice edged in sadness. "I was hoping you could tell me."

"What do you mean? I haven't seen him at school lately and heard he was out sick with a bad virus." The timing of his virus and our breakup was too coincidental; I'd suspected he was faking an illness to avoid seeing me. I mean, our breakup had been *that* bad. Worse than bad—apocalyptic.

"You're into the occult, the work of the devil," he'd accused me after catching me summoning ghosts at a séance. "I can never forgive that."

That was over three weeks ago. When Josh walked out that day, I knew it was really over for us. I should have felt sad ... but I didn't. Instead I was relieved, and hopeful that we'd both be happier now. Josh would hook up with a nice normal girl who applauded his magic tricks and didn't see ghosts or have telepathic conversations with her spirit guide. And finally, I was free to give my heart to Dominic.

Still, our break-up left me with an unfinished feeling, like when you walk out of a movie before the final scene. I wanted to explain to Josh that being psychic was an important part of me and had nothing to do with black magic. But he hadn't returned any of my messages.

And now his mother was calling…

"Josh isn't sick—at least I hope not. He's…he's—" Mrs. DeMarco cut off with a sob. "Gone."

"Gone?" I tensed. "For how long?"

"Over a week. He left a note telling us not to worry, but there's no word from him and I—" Her voice broke. "I don't know what to do."

"What about the police?"

"They wouldn't even put out one of those missing kids alerts for him because he left a note. They say he's a runaway."

"Not Josh. He's one of the most responsible, reliable people I know."

"That's what I told the police. But even my husband wants to wait for Josh to come home on his own. But what if he's hurt or sick and needs help? I've waited long enough. I have to try to find him, so I'm calling his friends."

As I wondered if Josh's disappearance could somehow be my fault, I realized there was silence on Mrs. DeMarco's end. Thinking I'd lost the connection—and feeling a teensy bit glad to bring this awkward conversation to an end—I was about to hang up when Mrs. DeMarco suddenly blurted out, "I—I understand you and Josh broke up."

5

"Uh, yeah," I replied cautiously. How much did she know? Had Josh told his mother I worshipped the devil and practiced black magic? I knew, from past experience, that some people weren't cool with paranormal stuff.

"He didn't say why," Josh's mother replied. "I realize this is none of my business, but was he upset when you broke up? Upset enough to ... to hurt himself, or—"

"Oh my god, no! Josh would never do anything like that," I insisted. Josh has been upset, all right, but he wasn't suicidal. Especially since he'd been the one to dump me, not the other way around. Yet why did I feel so guilty?

"If you have any information at all, you must tell me," Josh's mother said firmly, almost as if she were the psychic one. "Even if things between you and my son ended badly, I know that deep down, you still care about him."

"I swear I'd tell you if I knew anything."

"You may know more than you realize. Would you come over so we can talk in person?"

"You mean ... *now*?"

"If you don't mind. Besides, it'll do Horse good to see you. That impossible dog won't eat since Josh left. I've tried four vets and none of them have helped. Horse is always so excited to see you. Maybe you can convince him to eat."

"He's a great dog," I admitted. "I've missed him."

"So you'll come over right away?" she asked hopefully.

"Well ... okay." A thought came to me. "I have this

friend who is really amazing with animals and might be able to help Horse. Is it okay if I bring him?"

"Of course. Is he a vet?"

"No. But he understands animals so well that you'd think he was actually talking to them."

Then I hung up, and went to find Dominic.

*   *   *

It was an unusually frigid morning for northern California, wintry breaths of air puffing across the slate-blue sky and frost sparkling in ice crystals on fences, trees, and vehicles, transforming our rundown farmhouse into a Christmas card scene. Even my grandmother's dented secondhand sedan glimmered like a holiday gift.

I wrapped a jacket over my sweatshirt as I stepped onto the porch. The screen door banged behind me, not quite shutting, so I reached back to close it securely. My footsteps crunched on frosty weeds as I crossed the yard and I held out my arms for balance so I wouldn't slip and fall, which would be humiliating if anyone was around to see. But there were only horses, cows, geese, and chickens. Even my cat Lilybelle wasn't spying from the porch rail as usual, but content to stay inside by the wood stove.

Dominic's truck was parked in its spot on the side of the barn. Its frosted windows reminded me of a scary-wonderful night when we'd been stranded in a snowstorm, huddling inside the truck for warmth. It was one of those pivotal life moments when everything was suddenly as clear as the sun breaking through gray clouds. And I knew that Dominic was the one for me … and Josh wasn't.

Since then I'd been smiling a lot.

It was hard to believe it had only been a few months since Dominic had come to live and work on my grandmother's farm, accompanied by his falcon Dagger and shrouded in mystery. It was loathing at first sight for me. Dominic was rude, and I resented how my grandmother treated him like a long-lost son rather than an employee.

He messed with my emotions, which complicated my relationship with Josh—who was so perfect that I was flattered he'd chosen me for a girlfriend. Dominic was the opposite of perfect, and so damn secretive I still wasn't sure about his last name. But he was like a sliver under my skin that I couldn't ignore. And he won me over with his kindness to animals, unconditional loyalty to Nona, and quiet interest in literature.

He kissed great, too.

Dominic's supernatural connection to animals was only one of the reasons I sought him out now. The other reasons were completely personal and included thoughts that made my cheeks burn. Visualizing his gentle, rugged face, and imagining the rough-yet-soft touch of his hands, sent my emotions rocketing.

He lived in the barn loft, which sounded primitive until you stepped into the spacious, gleaming, wood-floored room with its large picture windows, high wood-beamed ceiling, antique furniture, bathroom, and kitchenette. Nona called the rustic décor "pioneer modern." The loft had originally been used by her third (or fourth?) husband as an artist's studio. The paint smells had long faded, and I couldn't imagine anyone other than Dominic living here.

I climbed the steps leading up to the loft and tapped on the door. When I called Dominic's name, there was no answer or sound of footsteps. I turned the knob and stepped inside. The room was empty—even the wooden pedestal by the window where Dagger usually perched.

"Dominic?" I called, in the direction of the bathroom.

The door was cracked open and I listened for sounds of running water in case he was showering. But there was silence. So I peeked inside the bathroom, misty warmth enveloping me. A damp towel was draped over the shower door, evidence that Dominic had recently been here. And I got this mental image of Dominic wearing nothing but a towel, smiling at me in a way that could lead ... well, somewhere I wasn't ready for yet. We'd agreed to take things slowly, to just enjoy being together.

Guessing he'd gotten up early to tend the livestock, I left the loft and checked the out-buildings and animal pens, even the stinky pig enclosure. Still no sign of Dominic. I was starting to worry until I caught a flash of movement far away, at the border of my grandmother's property where dense woods sprawled for acres.

9

A horseback rider.

I recognized Dominic's muscular shoulders and sandy-brown hair, and the comfortable-yet-totally-in-control way he sat a saddle. With an admiring sigh, I leaned against a fence rail, watching.

Dominic rode Rio, the youngest of my grandmother's horses, a dusky-brown, six-year-old Arabian gelding. They galloped with such natural grace, as if man and horse were one being. Their stride quickened—rising and falling, flying across the hard dirt pasture with dust puffing behind them like dark smoke. Although I was used to Dominic's uncanny skill with animals, I was awed all over again. Just like Dominic connected psychically with animals, we'd connected, too, and he seemed to understand me better than anyone ever had. I wanted to know more about him, too, but he'd had a violent childhood and was reluctant to talk about his past.

He was too far away right now for eye contact, but I sensed the instant he became aware of me. Just like that, he knew I was watching and I knew he knew. He clasped the reins in one hand and waved with the other. Then he spun the horse in a slow, graceful arc—showing off. Laughing, I applauded, and climbed high on the fence to wave back.

Rider and horse galloped toward me, closer and closer until I could see Dominic's grin. He leaned over to say something to Rio, then the horse flicked its tail and pranced to a smooth stop a few yards from where I waited at the fence.

"Hey," Dominic said in his usual short-on-words way. It used to annoy me, but now I could read between the lines.

"I need to talk to you," I told him.

"Sure." He patted the horse but his gaze stayed with me. "Wait while I tend to Rio."

I slipped down off the fence, admiring Dominic's gentle way of murmuring to the horse as he unfastened the bridle and slipped off the saddle. I couldn't hear what he was saying as he rubbed down Rio's sweaty back, but obviously Rio understood, because he swished his brown tail as if offering thanks.

Only after Dominic had given Rio a bucket of oats and led him to a trough of water did he finally return to me.

"Sabine," he said, clasping my hands in his calloused palms and pulling me close.

It was so natural, effortless, and I was a perfect fit in his arms, as if we'd been together in past lives. He lifted my chin with a gentle touch of his thumb, then whispered my name again as he tilted my face to meet his. As his lips caressed mine, the world seemed to stop. Sounds and worries faded away until I was only aware of Dominic ... and then reality came rushing back.

"Dominic, I had a frantic call from Mrs. DeMarco," I said, reluctantly pulling away. "She's worried about Josh," "Josh DeMarco?" Dominic scowled. There was no love lost between my ex and current boyfriends.

"He's gone off somewhere."

"Good for him."

"But not good for his family—or his dog," I added with a grim shake of my head. "Horse won't eat anything."

"Oh." Dominic's hostility changed to concern. "That could get serious."

When I explained that Mrs. DeMarco could use some help with Horse, Dominic was already moving, pulling his keys from his pocket and gesturing for me to head toward his truck. I hurried after him and hopped up into the passenger seat. On the drive to Josh's upscale neighborhood, I told Dominic the little I knew about Horse's condition,

Ten minutes later, Dominic braked hard, sliding a few feet on the icy pavement before parking crookedly in front of Josh's house. He jumped out and slammed the door, then came around to my door to give me a hand. While I loved holding his hand, it seemed kind of weird right in front of my ex-boyfriend's house, so I paused to adjust my jacket zipper.

My gaze drifted to the two-story house next to the DeMarco's—and I caught movement at a window. But then I blinked, and saw only a still curtain. Yet the prickles on my skin warned someone had been watching. I had a good idea who: Evan Marshall, Josh's best friend and my worst enemy.

But if Evan wanted to waste his time spying, that was his problem. I turned and caught up with Dominic, on the porch, just as the door was opening.

"Thank you for coming," Mrs. DeMarco said, taking my arm as she led us inside her home. She was pale without her usual cherry-red lipstick, blush, and mascara. Her hair was tossed back in a ponytail instead of smoothed in a stylish chignon. I quickly introduced her to Dominic.

"He understands animals better than anyone I know," I added.

"I've tried everything and nothing works."

Dominic would think of something, I assured her.

I still found it hard to believe that Josh would abandon his dog. He loved Horse so much that he kept doggy pictures in his wallet and, instead of dinner-and-a-movie-dates, we had often picnicked and played Frisbee at a dog park.

Mrs. DeMarco guided us through the living room and kitchen to the double glass door leading into the backyard. "It's so pitiful to watch that sweet dog lie there like he's dying. He won't eat or do anything."

Dominic wasted no time going outside to see Horse, but I lingered in the doorway, waiting to talk privately with Mrs. DeMarco. She just stood there, one hand pressed against the glass door, her expression distant. I had a strong feeling she was thinking of Josh.

I focused on this feeling, staring deeply into her face to an aura bleeding with blazing reds, oranges, and jaded greens, all swirling in a pattern of fear.

Then, with no warning, my world shifted and blurred. I was yanked from my physical self, whirling dizzily like dust in a cyclone and flung far away from my physical body. I was flying, in a blur of faceless souls and buzzing whispers.

When everything slowed down, I was no longer with Josh's mother.

Instead, I saw Josh.

He stood by a window. Outside, pines disappeared into clouds, but inside, a fireplace warmed a large rustic room with heavy wood furniture. Candles flickered. In the background, cloaked figures huddled around the crackling flames in a brick fireplace, their voices low in intense conversation.

Josh's hair was slicked back from his face in an old-fashioned style. He was dressed like he was going to a costume party, in fancy black slacks, a blue silky shirt with flowing sleeves, and a black velvet vest. He cradled an ornate knife in his hands almost reverently, turning it over and over with an intense expression, as if meditating.

As he murmured strange, foreign-sounding words, Josh's gaze focused on the knife. He was completely absorbed, his eyes shining, entranced. Then he slowly lifted the knife high over his head. The sharp silver tip reflected orange-red fire and wavered in the air.

Then, with a fierce lunge, Josh jerked the knife inward. And stabbed the blade into his chest.

2

Dizzy and breathless, I slammed back into my physical body, gripping the sliding glass door with white-knuckled hands. Only seconds had passed during my vision.

"Sabine, what's wrong?" Mrs. DeMarco put her arm gently around my shoulders. "You're shaking."

"I'm okay. I just ... um ..." I could *not* explain about astral travel and psychic visions to Josh's mother. "I get dizzy when I forget to eat."

"You poor child. My mother had low blood sugar

problems and couldn't skip meals either without getting sick. Here, this should help." She picked up a bowl of fresh fruit from the counter and held it out to me.

I'd missed breakfast and was a little hungry, so I took an apple. Josh's mother was watching me with concern, so after taking a few bites, I assured her I felt much better.

But that wasn't true—I was terrified for Josh.

My visions usually foretold the future or offered glimpses into the past. A few months ago, after I'd had a premonition of a bloody dragonfly tattoo, I'd met a girl with the exact tattoo. And recently, while sleeping, I'd astral-traveled to spy on my "surprise-you-have-a-half-sister" Jade. (All I knew about Jade was that we shared a father and looked enough alike to be twins. Naturally, we'd hated each other at first, but we got to know each other better after my psychic skills helped solve a murder that happened at her home.)

Yet my vision about Josh wasn't like anything I'd ever experienced. He didn't look like himself, draped in that old-fashioned costume as if attending a masquerade party. Then again, a party might explain the cloaked figures by the fireplace. But with all those people in the room, why hadn't someone stopped Josh from stabbing himself?

Setting the apple down on the kitchen counter, I turned to Mrs. DeMarco. "You wanted to talk about Josh," I reminded.

"I've already talked to most of his friends, and no one

knows anything. I hoped you might think of something Josh said or that you heard from someone else."

I shook my head. My friends knew better than to mention Josh. Well, except for Penny-Love, self-proclaimed queen of gossip. Last week she'd told me a crazy rumor about Josh being so sick that the government had quarantined him in a secret underground hospital. Then her artsy boyfriend Jacques got on the topic of pandemics and said all of Josh's friends should be quarantined, too. He actually pulled out a paper and asked me for names! But I shut him up by pointing out that Penny-Love was one of Josh's friends and she'd have to be quarantined, too.

"I honestly don't know anything," I told Mrs. DeMarco. "Exactly how long has Josh been gone?"

"Eight days." Tears streamed down her cheeks.

I gently led her to the table and sat her down in a wooden chair. I offered her a paper napkin to dry her eyes, then sat beside her, leaning forward in my chair and giving her a solemn look. "Please tell me what happened."

Mrs. DeMarco dabbed her eyes with the napkin. "In Josh's note, he told us not to look for him. His father and I assumed he'd return in a few days. I didn't want his grades to suffer, so I covered for him by telling the school he was sick and picking up his assignments. Every time the phone rang, I was sure it would be Josh. But it's been over a week and still nothing. I'm afraid ... afraid that something happened to him."

"Josh didn't say where he was going?"

"No."

"His car's still here, so he must have left with a friend. Any idea who?"

"Arturo."

"Amazing Arturo?" Josh was apprenticed to the famous magician.

"His note said he was with Arturo, but not where they'd gone. I keep wondering if I did something to make him leave..." Her voice cracked and I worried that she'd break down. Ever since losing her oldest son tragically in a car accident, Mrs. DeMarco was very protective of Josh.

"Don't blame yourself—it isn't your fault," I assured her. But it might be mine, I thought, remembering Josh's final words to me. Had he been heart-broken enough to run away? Was I responsible for his mother's tears?

"Why hasn't he called?" Mrs. DeMarco asked. "Evan hasn't even heard anything and those boys are closer than brothers. What if my Josh was attacked, or is lying hurt somewhere without anyone around to help him? At first I was sure Josh would come home, since he didn't take his car, phone, or laptop. But after a week... I don't know what to think."

"Did you call Arturo?"

"Of course. No one answered, so my husband and I drove to his house." The lines in her face seemed deeper, as if she was aging before my eyes.

"What happened?"

"The house was closed up. None of the neighbors had seen either Arturo or his wife and had no idea where they'd gone. I wanted to report Josh missing but his father said we couldn't force Josh to come home, that we need to trust him to come back on his own. I trust Josh, but I don't trust Arturo."

I didn't trust Arturo either.

And I couldn't shake the vision of that silver knife. Was it a glimpse into something that had already happened or a warning about the future? If it was a warning, then was there still time to change the vision and save Josh?

"Mrs. DeMarco, can I see the note?"

"Why?" She wiped her eyes.

"Because I'm worried, too."

"I'll get it for you."

After she left the room, I went over to the sliding glass door and looked out into the backyard. Dominic was crawling on his hands like a dog. Horse lifted his floppy ears as he watched Dominic wag his head in some sort of doggy communication. Then Dominic bent down to the dog bowl and ... *ew* gross!

Dominic was eating doggy kibble.

I started to go outside, but stopped when I heard footsteps behind me.

"Here," Mrs. DeMarco gave me the folded paper. "Go ahead and read it, although it doesn't say much."

I unfolded the lined sheet of paper and looked down at the short, hand-written message:

Going with Arturo. Take care of Horse.
Do not look for me.
Love, Josh.

I turned the note over, hoping for more, but only found blank paper.

"I told you it wasn't much help." Mrs. DeMarco rubbed her forehead as if getting a headache. "It doesn't say where they went or how long they would be gone, or why all the secrecy."

"Everything about the Amazing Arturo is secret," I said bitterly, remembering all the silences from Josh whenever Arturo's name came up. I'd never met Josh's mentor, but I knew that Arturo was inducting Josh into a mysterious world of magicians. Josh had even gotten a tattoo with the initials PFC and refused to tell me what it meant.

Stepping away from Josh's mother, I studied the note. The handwriting looked like his, but Josh wasn't usually so inconsiderate of his parents. He'd confided to me that his parents still had trouble dealing with the death of his brother, so he tried to be there for them. He didn't complain or rebel when they were overprotective, and was always considerate and respectful. Leaving with no warning was very un-Joshlike.

Running my fingers over his written words, I closed

my eyes and tried to summon a vision. But I got nothing. My psychic skills didn't come with an *On Demand* feature. How ironic that I couldn't predict my own predictions. What was the use in being psychic if I couldn't control this ability?

For a long time, I'd rebelled against this gift. I ignored my visions, pretending that the dark strip in my blond hair wasn't the mark of a seer and that I was a normal girl. I was accepted into the "cool" group at school, had a cheerleader for a best friend, and dated ultra-popular Josh. But I couldn't go on faking and lying to myself, so I'd finally embraced my talents and was glad when my gift could help someone. Still, not being able to access my skills when I wanted to made me crazy.

Did you forget to ask me? a sassy voice said in my head.

"Opal?" I asked without speaking, since my spirit guide could hear my thoughts. Closing my eyes, I envisioned her tawny skin, regal upswept black hair, and critical, arched dark brows. "You're here?"

I'm always nearby even if my presence isn't obvious to those who merely have eyes and not a sight for the beyond, she said.

A simple "yes" would have done. But then, Opal never made things simple. "Can you help me find Josh?"

Help has a wide abundance of meanings, and for the doors to answers to be opened, you'll need to journey along the right path toward a destination unimagined.

As usual, she was confusing me. "What door and path?"

When you wrinkle your forehead like that it makes you look old.

"A three-hundred-year-old ghost is telling *me* I'm old?"

Do not show your impertinence, young lady, and adhere closely to my advice if you wish to gain insight into the matters that trouble you.

"Josh is missing. Please, just help me find him."

Suggest to this woman that it could be enlightening for you to examine her son's room.

Huh? I had to think for a minute to figure out what Opal meant. Sometimes I wondered if we were speaking the same language.

"Mrs. DeMarco," I said, turning around. "Would you mind if I looked in Josh's room?"

"Why?" She pushed a loose strand of light-brown hair from her face.

"There might be a clue about where he's gone."

"I've already searched and found nothing. All he left was this note." She held out her hand. "May I have it back?"

Nodding, I gave her the paper. She cradled it in her palm, running her fingertips over it, then folding it twice and tucking it away in a skirt pocket.

"If I look at Josh's room, I might remember something he said that could help find him. I promise to be quick."

"Thank you for caring." Her gaze drifted toward the backyard. "While you're doing that, I'll go outside to check on your friend. Am I seeing things, or is he crawling inside Horse's dog house?"

"Dominic is really hands-on when it comes to animals."

While she went outside, I walked down the hall, passing the family room where Josh and I had watched DVDs on their big screen TV and played video games. Despite our break-up, I still considered him a friend. He might hate me now, but all I felt was sadness ... and fear.

Josh's room looked the same as ever, only neater—there were fresh vacuum grooves in the nut-brown carpet and I smelled the scent of flowery air-freshener. One wall was covered with posters of basketball stars and another had a tall shelf with sports trophies and framed photos of friends and family. I recognized a heart-breaking picture of Josh with his brother, probably taken just months before the accident. There was also a picture of a distinguished bald man in a black velvet, silver-trimmed suit, standing beside a slim, blond woman who seemed to fade into the background. Could they be the Amazing Arturo and his wife?

I continued with my search, checking Josh's backpack, which held nothing out of the ordinary. Hanging on a wall hook were leashes for walking Horse. I'd done this a lot with Josh, and usually ended up laughing when Horse galloped ahead and we had to run to keep up with him.

So much of Josh's life was in this room ... minus Josh.

After searching drawers and the closet and crawling to peer under the bed, I had to give up. There were no hidden clues about Josh's connection to Arturo. The only "magical" thing I found, in a box underneath a rainbow clown wig and a pair of big floppy shoes, was a gaudy magic wand encircled with plastic jewels and a fake diamond tip.

If this wand was magic, then I was Houdini.

Still, there was an odd aura about the wand. As I held it, warmth spread through my fingers until it pounded like thunder in my head and everything darkened, shapes shifting. In my mind, I saw a beautiful woman. She had dark sapphire eyes and golden skin, and her gleaming copper hair was clipped back in a gold barrette so that it rained like a flaming waterfall down her back. She stood on a polished wood podium, maybe a stage. She wore a jeweled vest over pink silk that reminded me of how harem girls dress in old movies. She spun in a pirouette like a dancer, then waved a jeweled wand over an oblong wooden box—a coffin. In a puff of blue smoke, the coffin lid opened and a hand rose from inside, waving a handkerchief. I heard applause, and realized this woman wasn't merely a dancer—she was a magician.

Then the image vanished and I was simply holding a cheap imitation of the jeweled wand from my vision, standing in my ex-boyfriend's room, confused. Who was the woman and what was her connection to Josh?

"Opal," I said out loud, "I could use some help here."

Lift your gaze to look beyond the curtain of your own expectations.

"Beyond what curtain? English, please."

Your knowledge of English is far removed from the actuality of its original form, but I'm willing to overlook your limitations. You're overlooking the obvious, too, expecting to find answers in inanimate objects instead of following the breath of a living path. The bonds of birth are more binding than you realize, but the answers come when the bonds are freed and hearts are opened.

That had to be the most illogical nonsense I'd ever heard. If Opal had a solid body, I'd throw something at her.

Instead, I thought about her words. Her phrase about a "curtain" made me lift my gaze to the dark blue curtain covering the only window in Josh's room.

The curtains didn't close all the way, and I could see the dark green of the Marshall's house next door.

Hmmm ... what did Evan know about Josh? Was that what Opal was hinting? I wouldn't put it past Evan to lie to the DeMarcos. I'll bet he knew exactly where Josh had gone. Evan Marshall didn't care if Horse mourned himself to death or if the DeMarcos were sick with worry—he only cared about himself.

As I watched, the front door opened and Evan stepped onto the porch, turning to reach for someone behind him. Pulling the curtain wider, I saw a girl slipping into Evan's arms, her long wavy red hair jarring me with recognition. I couldn't see her face, only her slender back as she leaned into Evan, their arms entwining. She molded herself against his chest, their faces closing together, kissing.

When she turned, I saw her face.

A face very much like mine.

My half-sister, Jade.

3

I blinked a few times to make sure I wasn't hallucinating. But that *was* my half-sister locking lips with my arch-enemy. She hadn't once mentioned Evan in her texts.

How long had this been going on?

Last month, when Jade had flirted with Evan on the horseback ride/campout, I'd thought she was just hitting on him to annoy me. It worked, too. But we'd survived some scary moments together and gotten past our problems. Jade had admitted to being jealous of me and I confessed that

I had jealousy issues, too, because she was actually Dad's eldest daughter instead of me. After the campout, Dad did some confessing as well, telling Mom about his "secret" daughter—which erupted in lots of drama. But living over a hundred miles away on Nona's farm made it easy for me to stay out of that, and privately I tried to forge a friendship with Jade through texts and email. We talked about school, friends, and our mutual interest in fencing.

I'd thought everything was cool with us. Guess not.

I hated Jade for lying. Even more, I hated myself for believing her.

Well, I'd had enough of her lies. I stomped out of Josh's room. I sped up, running through the hall and the living room. The front door banged behind me and I stood for a moment, shivering. But the shock of the chilly air couldn't compare to my raging emotions. I stormed across the path connecting the two homes, not realizing I was still holding Josh's cheesy plastic wand until I saw it in my hand. Cheap and fake—just like my half-sister. Slipping the wand into a pocket in my jacket, I stopped abruptly several feet away from the embracing couple.

"Jade."

I barely whispered her name but it had the effect of a lightning strike, slashing across the lawn with a force startling enough to split them apart.

"Sabine!" Jade's cheeks reddened until they were almost as bright as her hair. "What are you doing here?"

"Trespassing," Evan spat out, reaching out for Jade possessively. "Get out."

"I'll leave after I talk to my *half*-sister." I emphasized "half" like I was swearing.

"Sabine, this isn't a good time," Jade said, with a sharpness that stung. "We'll talk later, okay?"

"No, it's not okay. Can't you tell the truth about you and Evan? I thought we were ... well ... you know."

"My relationship with Evan isn't about you."

"You told me you were dating a guy from your fencing class. Evan doesn't even go to your school."

"So I lied." Jade shrugged. "No big deal."

"It is to me."

"I knew you'd overreact, just like you are now. That's why I didn't tell you." Her words came out tough, but her gaze softened. "It's not like I expected to see you here."

"I didn't expect to see you, either," I accused her. "Your last text said you had so much homework you were staying home this weekend—over a hundred miles away."

"And yours said you were going Christmas shopping." She gave a sarcastic sweep of her arms. "Kind of far from the mall, aren't you? Were you spying on me again?"

I flinched at the "again," since when I first learned Dad had a secret daughter, I'd spied on Jade.

"I was not spying," I retorted, lifting my chin as if I didn't care what she said or thought of me. "I was at the DeMarcos' and just happened to look out the window."

"The DeMarcos'?" Evan stepped toward me with a ferocious glare. "What were you doing there?"

"Mrs. DeMarco invited me."

"You're lying! She wouldn't."

"Yes, she did. She's worried about Josh and wanted my help."

"That's crap. You're the last person she'd want around—not after what you did."

"I didn't do anything, except try to help—which is more than you're doing." A swift wind lashed against me but I stood my ground. "If anyone knows where Josh is, you should, but you haven't told his parents."

"I'm not the one who drove Josh away." Evan pointed at me.

"Josh was the one who broke up with me—not the other way around!"

"Getting defensive, are you? Well, you deserve to feel guilty. You pushed him too far. He had you up on this pedestal, insisting you were a sweet, wonderful girl. I warned him, but would he listen to his best friend? No, he believed you. When he found out I was right, that you'd been lying to him, he was destroyed."

"I never meant to hurt him. I tried to explain."

"Explain what? That you're a lying, cheating bitch?"

"Ev, that's harsh." Jade tugged on Evan's arm. "Stop already and let's go inside. I'm getting cold."

"I'm sick of everyone believing her lies." Evan spit

out the words. "Careful, Jade, or your twisted half-sister will screw you over, too. Do you have any idea what sick shit she's into? Josh caught her summoning evil spirits at a séance."

I shot Jade a look, but she quickly glanced away without answering. Guess she hadn't mentioned to Evan that my grandmother had arranged the séance for her. The not-at-all-evil-spirit who'd been summoned had been her beloved stepfather.

"I had nothing to do with Josh's leaving," I insisted. "He left with Arturo."

"To get away from you." Evan spat.

I stumbled back, as if slapped. I didn't believe that ... didn't want to believe it.

"You're to blame." Evan tightened his hands into fists like he wanted to slam me. "And now you have the nerve to say I'm lying, that I would hurt my best friend's family? His family is my family, too. You dated Josh for a few months but I've been his friend since we were kids. I went through hell with him after his brother died. I know him better than anyone."

"Exactly!" I exclaimed, pointing my finger right back at him. "You know him so well, you must know where he is."

"Shifting blame won't get you off this time," Evan warned. "I never told anyone at school about your freaky habits out of respect for Josh. I don't have any reason to hold back now. I'll tell everyone you're a heartless witch."

"Lighten up, Ev." Jade reached out, touching Evan's arm. "Sabine *is* my sister."

"The half-sister spoiled princess you can't stand. Isn't that what you told me?"

"Well ... I didn't exactly ..."

"Jade?" Hurt scorched through me. "You said that?"

"Not in those ... well ... I didn't mean to—"

"What exactly did you mean?" I interrupted.

"I plead the fifth." Jade folded her arms across her chest.

Her reply, which was clearly meant to remind me we shared the same attorney father, made me so angry I could hardly speak.

Evan slipped his arm around Jade, pulling her close. "Let it go, Jade. She doesn't matter. Nothing really does except bringing Josh back home."

The genuine sadness in his tone startled me. "You really don't know where he is?" I asked.

"If I did, he'd be back already." Evan's hostility slipped again and his aura flashed with sad shades of yellow and purple, as if his psyche was bruised. "If you really are psychic, look into your crystal ball or whatever freaky thing you do to find him."

"You don't believe in psychics," I said sarcastically.

"I don't, especially you. But Josh has been gone for too long and that's just not like him. If you have some sort of freaky power that can find him, then go ahead and prove me wrong."

"I can't just make things happen."

"Exactly what a fake would say."

"I don't care what you think."

"You should," he threatened with renewed hostility. "If Josh isn't home by Christmas, I'll make sure everyone at school knows about your black magic rituals and how you used voodoo to kill that football player at your last school. When I'm done, you won't have any friends—not even that hot cheerleader you hang out with."

I wanted to argue that Penny-Love was my BFF and would stand by me no matter what. But I'd never told her about my psychic ability and she could be a little shallow when it came to popularity. I didn't hold that against her, understanding too well what it was like not to fit in. Being psychic ruined my reputation at my last school, and all my friends—even my very best friend—had turned against me.

And it could happen again.

4

When Evan pulled Jade into his house, she wouldn't look at me. She simply went along with him, proving that my first impression of her had been right. She might be half a sister, but she wasn't even a fraction of a friend.

The door slammed shut.

Chilled inside and out, I wrapped my arms around myself. But no matter how tight I held on, emotionally I was falling apart. Evan had accused me of the thing I'd secretly feared; that I was to blame for Josh's disappearance. If something terrible happened to Josh, it would be my fault.

Slowly, I turned back toward the DeMarcos' house, trying to figure out a way to make things right. I thought about what I knew:

- Josh had gone off somewhere with Arturo over a week ago.
- He hadn't taken his phone, clothes, or laptop.
- He told his parents not to look for him.
- Evan didn't know where he was.
- I had a vision of him in a rustic building with cloaked strangers.
- The knife. (Didn't want to think what this meant.)

I sighed, feeling even more confused.

I'd only taken a few steps when I heard Dominic shout something from the DeMarcos' backyard.

Alarmed, I raced to the side gate and sprinted into the backyard. There was Dominic by the dog house. He turned toward me, a triumphant smile on his face.

"Check it out." He pointed to Horse, who stood up on his four gangling legs and wagged his tail as he ate from his dog bowl.

"He's eating!" I rejoiced.

"Cool, huh?"

"More than cool. You're amazing." I stepped toward Dominic, smiling. He opened his arms and I fell into them, holding tight. He hugged back with such warmth that my body temperature rose. We shared a look, sort of a bookmark to hold our place so we could come back to this moment when we were alone.

Stepping away, I reached over to rub behind Horse's ears. The dog wagged his tail and kept on crunching his food. Dominic went over to the back door and called Mrs. DeMarco. When she came out and saw that Horse was eating, she gasped with surprise.

"You did it! Oh my god, I can hardly believe it. You're a miracle worker!" she told Dominic.

"I didn't do much." Dominic shrugged as if embarrassed. "Keep an eye on him and give him a lot of attention, and he should be okay."

"I can't thank you enough," she said. She offered to pay Dominic what she would have paid a veterinarian, but Dominic refused.

"Seeing this dog healthy is enough for me," he said.

We said our good-byes, then left the backyard.

I climbed into Dominic's truck and fastened my seat belt. I was feeling great until my gaze drifted to the Marshall house again. Then all Evan's accusations rushed back, ruining my mood. Jade and Evan together, united against me. God, I hated Evan. He was more toxic than an infectious disease. Jade would be sorry, too, because he'd dump her like all his other girlfriends. Evan (nicknamed "Moving On Marsh") had a rep as a player with a new girlfriend every week.

Dominic suggested we get something to eat, so we drove to a roadside taco truck. There were about half a dozen other cars parked in the graveled lot, which meant reasonable prices and great food. I swung open the car door and, my feet crunching on gravel, inhaled the mouthwatering aroma of carne asada, rice, and beans.

The line was long but the service quick. We returned to the warm, cozy truck and unwrapped our breakfast burritos. Dominic turned on the radio, switching it from his usual country station to my preferred alt rock station.

Biting into my burrito, I studied Dominic, thinking how being together felt so right and longing to freeze-frame this moment. He'd changed so much in the short time we'd known each other, his wall of reserve and suspicion coming down. He'd opened his heart up to me and I'd fallen inside.

A little red sauce dripped down Dominic's arm, and as he wiped it off, I admired his tanned, rough hands. It still surprised me how gently those callused fingers could caress my skin. Rough and gentle—that was my Dominic.

"Thanks," I told him simply.

"For what?" He arched his brow.

"For being you." I folded the burrito wrapper and tossed it in the garbage bag hanging near the truck's dashboard.

"Not many guys would have dropped everything to help their girlfriend's ex-boyfriend's dog."

Dominic shrugged. "Not a dog's fault who owns him."

"Animals always come first with you," I teased.

"Not only animals," he said, with a smile that made me wish we were alone in a romantic hideaway, not sitting in a truck cab in public. "I came today because you asked me to."

"I know, and it means a lot to me."

"You mean a lot to me."

Our eyes connected. Feelings swelled inside me in deep sweeping currents. I reached across the seat and squeezed his hand, imagining being with him alone... and much more. But this wasn't the time or the place. So I took a deep breath and shifted the conversation back to safe territory.

"You were great with Horse," I said in a casual tone. "But I nearly gagged when you ate the doggy kibble."

"To be honest, I was faking," he admitted, grimacing as if remembering something painful.

I got a flash of the younger Dominic, chained outside and bruised from beatings by his uncle. The only food his uncle had given him was dog food—which he'd refused. I'd seen this memory already and knew Dominic had suffered horrible indignities before running away. I still didn't know everything he'd gone through, but I knew enough to understand why the one thing he would never eat was dog food.

"Well, what you did was impressive," I said in a cheerful tone to lighten the moment. "Mrs. DeMarco said you succeeded where all those vets failed. She would have written you a big check—you could charge a lot as a dog miracle worker."

"When everything is about money, life is not worth anything. Like Emerson said: *money often costs too much.*"

"But you'll need money for your horse-shoeing business," I argued, always impressed when Dominic quoted famous dead people. Not only was my boyfriend hot-looking and considerate, he read literature for fun. "You'd rather work for yourself than someone else, and extra money could start up your business."

"I don't take money for helping a friend."

I knew he didn't mean Mrs. DeMarco. Horse was his friend. Placing my hand gently on his arm, I nodded to show I understood. "I'm just glad Horse is better."

"But he might relapse if Josh doesn't return." Dominic started the truck and gravel sputtered as we pulled onto the road. "Horse is anxious about Josh."

"He told you that?"

"Yeah, although not in actual words. In a mind-picture he showed me his leash and Josh, which meant he missed going for walks with Josh. Then there was an image of Josh driving off in a sports car, leaving Horse behind."

"Horse saw Josh drive away?" I asked, grabbing onto

the armrest when Dominic made a sharp turn down a country road lined with vineyards. "Did he see Arturo?"

"All I picked up was a quick flash of a young guy with a blond ponytail."

"But Arturo is bald. So if he didn't go with Arturo, who did he go with? What else did Horse tell you?"

"He didn't like the blond guy's smell."

"Bad body odor? Aftershave?"

"Not that kind of smell." Dominic shook his head. "Compare it to how you see colored auras of a person's emotions. Horse smelled *evil*."

I bit my lip, remembering the evil aura of a haunted witch ball I'd possessed (to be exact, the witch ball had possessed *me*.) I'd had rare brushes with people, too, with auras so dark that their souls sucked you in like a black hole. And then a memory clicked—of a tall, skeleton-like young man with a freakish white ponytail fleeing the scene of a crime.

"That's it!" I snapped my fingers.

"What?" Dominic tilted toward me curiously.

"I know who Josh left with!"

"Who?"

"Grey, his new magician pal. They were always going off for secret magician meetings that Josh wouldn't tell me about."

Frowning, I remembered my first encounter with Grey, the vandal who'd smashed up Trick or Treats with a baseball bat. Trick or Treats was a wonderful little candy shop owned by my grandmother's friend Velvet, and I'd heard the awful smashes from the back room where we were gathered for a séance. I dashed outside and chased the vandal, but he drove away. I didn't realize the vandal and Grey were the same person until the day Josh and I broke up. I'd warned Josh that Grey was dangerous, but he refused to believe me.

And now Josh was missing.

Dominic didn't say anything for a few miles and I wondered if it had been a bad idea to talk about Josh. Discussing your ex is probably #1 on the *What Not to Say to Your New Boyfriend* list. I didn't want Dominic to think I still had feelings for Josh, because I so did *not*. But I liked him as a friend and it was natural to worry about a missing friend. Then, as I was thinking of some way to reassure Dominic that he was the only one for me, he suddenly glanced over and said the last thing in the universe I expected to hear from him.

"Sabine, I'm going to search for Josh."

Good thing I wasn't driving or we would have run off the road and smashed through a fence. "You want to find my ex-boyfriend?"

"Someone has to," Dominic said in a matter-of-fact way. "It sounds like Josh has got himself into a bad situation. If he doesn't return, Horse will starve himself to death."

"Finding Josh won't be easy." I twisted a loose strand

of my hair around my finger. "He doesn't want to be found. He's far away with cloaked strangers."

Dominic gave me a sharp, sideways look. "You had a vision?"

He knew me so well. So I told him about the cloaked figures and the knife.

"So Josh may be dead?" Dominic asked when I finished.

"No! He's okay...he has to be," I said, trying to convince myself. "Still, something bad could happen, so I asked his mother if I could look around his room."

"Did you find anything?"

"Oh, I found out something all right. But not inside Josh's bedroom." I tightened the hair strand around my finger so tight it snapped. "And not about Josh."

Dominic raised his brows in a question. I so didn't want to talk about the ugly scene with Jade and Evan. But this was Dominic and I could trust him, so I told him everything...well almost. I left out Evan's threat.

"Sabine, don't let your sister get to you. Sharing DNA doesn't mean you have to like each other."

"No chance of that now. I don't need her anyway. I already have two wonderful little sisters."

"Amy and Ashley are cool."

Mental note to self: call Amy and Ashley later and tell them just how much I appreciate them. Then I told Dominic about searching Josh's room.

"I touched some of his things, but couldn't sense where he was," I added.

"Finding is Thorn's talent, not yours," Dominic said matter-of-factly, referring to our Goth friend who had helped solve a few problems with her uncanny psychometry ability. All she had to do was touch an object for its energy to send off information like an automated GPS.

"Still, I should have picked up something," I complained. "All I got was Opal telling me to look through a curtain to find answers. Then I saw Jade ... well you know how badly that turned out."

"Your spirit guide may have been hinting that Jade knows something about Josh's disappearance."

"Jade only knows how to lie," I said bitterly.

"What about Evan? As Josh's best friend he may know where Josh went."

"I thought so at first, but not so much now."

Dominic drummed his fingers on the steering wheel. "We should ask Thorn to do her Finder thing in Josh's room."

I shook my head. "She won't do it. You know how weird Thorn gets about being psychic. She hates anyone making a big deal about it."

"She'd do it for you."

"You think?" I was never sure if Thorn really liked me. We didn't hang out at school or talk much. Still, we'd gone through some drama together and seemed to have some kind of bond.

"Thorn can't help find Josh unless we give her something of his to touch," Dominic added as he flipped the right blinker and turned down Nona's gravel driveway. "Which we don't have."

"Oh, don't we?" I pulled out the plastic wand from my jacket. I gave it a little wave and the diamond at the tip sparkled. It was like something a child would use to put on a pretend magic show. "How about this?"

"Where'd you get that?"

"Josh's room."

He grinned. "You amaze me."

His smile made my heart flutter, and I decided not to add that it was only by accident that I'd taken the wand.

Returning the wand to my jacket pocket, I grabbed my phone and texted Thorn, asking if we could stop by her house. Almost immediately I got a reply. Thorn said her house was a zoo of noisy siblings multiplied by their friends, so she'd meet us at Nona's.

I expected an empty driveway since my grandmother was away for the weekend, meeting with the CEO of a rival matchmaking business. So I was surprised to see the beat-up station wagon that Penny-Love often borrowed from her older brothers. Pen and I had talked about hitting the mall today, but not until this afternoon.

On the porch, Penny-Love was reaching for the door,

keys flashing silver in her hand. She turned toward us, her coppery ponytail bouncing.

"Sabine!" she called, coming to meet me as I stepped out of the truck.

"What are you doing here so early?"

"Nona is swamped with new clients so I offered to work a few extra hours." Penny-Love was a part-time "Love Assistant" for my grandmother's business, Soul-Mate Matches. "Besides, something's happened…"

"What?"

"Could you come inside with me?" I could see that her lips were trembling, as if she was close to crying. "I really need to talk. Privately."

She meant not in front of Dominic, so I turned to him. "Do you mind?"

"No prob. I've got chores to tend to." Dominic started to leave until Penny-Love called after him, "Wait!"

"What?" Dominic turned back, his brows raised.

"I almost forgot—a guy in a dark suit with a hideous orange tie was looking for you."

Dominic frowned. "He asked for me?"

"Not exactly, but you're the only Dominic I know. He was here when I showed up, and said he was a PI. I asked what he wanted and he said he was looking for Dominic Sarver. But your last name is Smith, at least that's what Sabine told me, so I said he had the wrong guy. Only he still wants to talk to you. Do know Dominic Sarver?"

"Never heard of him," he said.

"Well if you do, let him know the PI wants to talk about his uncle's death."

"Sure." Dominic didn't show any expression, but his aura swirled with dark, disturbing emotions as he walked away.

Penny-Love and I started toward the house but alarms were ringing in my psyche. Dominic had said he had chores, but he wasn't headed for the corral or livestock pens. He was going to the barn—to his loft room.

I stopped abruptly. "Pen, I just remembered something I have to tell Dominic. Go ahead, and I'll join you inside in a few minutes."

Then I hurried after Dominic, catching up with him as he was starting up the staircase to his loft apartment.

"What's wrong?" I demanded.

"Nothing."

"Don't lie to me. Your aura is insane with emotional colors."

"Sabine, go back to Pen." He didn't look at me, his expression like stone. "I have things to do."

"Your driver's license is fake, isn't it?" I guessed. "Your last name isn't Smith. It's Sarver."

He gripped the stair railing tightly, his gaze sweeping around the piles of hay, bags of feed, and animal pens.

"Dominic Andrew Sarver," he said after long seconds. "The PI was looking for me and he'll be back. Only I won't be here."

The way he spoke sounded so fatalistic, like he was never coming back.

"But you … you can't leave!" I gasped, shock quickly shifting to panic. "This is your home."

"Not anymore."

"But why?" My voice was breaking … along with my heart.

"My uncle didn't die naturally." Dominic pulled away from me. "I killed him."

5

I followed Dominic up the stairs.

"You can *not* leave."

He ignored me as if I wasn't there, hastily pulling open drawers and throwing clothes into a suitcase.

"Dominic, be reasonable. Your uncle beat you and chained you outside, treating you worse than an animal. Even if you did kill him, if you hadn't defended yourself, he would have killed you. You had no choice."

"My choice was to leave him ... dead."

"You were only a kid! It's amazing you even survived."

"I had help." Dominic looked up as the falcon fluttered down from his perch by the window then flew down to the corner of a dresser. He reached out to gently stroke the bird's glistening feathers, his gaze drifting back in time.

"What did Dagger have to do with it?" I asked, puzzled.

"I was chained up by the dog house and it was raining. My uncle taunted me by leaving only dog food. I told him I'd rather starve. I would have, too, except Dagger brought me food."

"Wow. He's even more amazing than I thought."

"I owe a lot to him."

"So let him keep living here. He's happy resting in the barn and hunting in the woods."

"I've been happy, too … more than I deserve." Dominic dropped his hand from the bird and crossed the room to his closet.

Before he could put more clothes to his suitcase, I moved quickly to block his way. "Listen, Dominic. Self-defense is a legal and moral defense. My dad's an attorney and I've heard him talk about cases not that different from yours. There was this ten-year-old girl he defended who stabbed her father when he was strangling her mother. It was ruled self-defense and all charges dropped. Dad's a great attorney. He'd represent you if I asked."

"No." Dominic scowled.

"But you need legal help. Running isn't any way to live."

"Neither is being caged behind bars."

"That won't ever happen with Dad on your side. He'll prove you're innocent."

"But I'm not. I did it." He pulled away from me, his shoulders drooping. "We fought. I hit him so hard he fell... and died. I just left him there. That's something I'll always have to live with. I was dumb to think that I could have a future and forget the past. I'll handle things my way."

"Can't you let someone help you just once?"

"I did... once. That's what brought me here."

"Nona," I guessed.

"Yeah. She told me she needed help around this place, and that if I let her teach me how to hone my psychic ability, I'd be helping her. I didn't really believe that but I came anyway. I figured I'd stay a few weeks or a month, then move on like always. What I didn't figure on was meeting you."

"Stay with me." I stepped closer, pulling his hand away from the suitcase and entwining my fingers in his, holding so tight he'd never go.

"You don't need my troubles."

"I want them. I'm part of them." I looked deeply into his eyes, willing him to love me enough to stay. "We can work this out together."

With his free hand, he stroked my hair gently. "Sabine,

you have no idea how much I—" His voice caught. "I want to stay."

"Then do it."

"It's complicated," he murmured, bringing my hand to his lips and softly kissing it. "I can't change the past."

Longing ached inside me. I wanted to beg and cry and threaten him—anything to make him stay.

"I'm not the only one who needs you," I said. "Nona relies on you."

"I've relied on her, too. More than you know," he added in a tone that hinted at secrets.

"What do you mean?"

"I was a scared kid when I met Nona, and she offered help without knowing anything about me."

"Wait a minute. Didn't you tell me that Nona knew your mother?"

"That's what she wanted me to say, since it made more sense than the truth."

"And the truth?" I persisted.

"We met when I was trying to find a home for my uncle's hunting dog. I wasn't the only one my uncle beat on. He kicked and half-starved Volcano. Your grandmother saved Volcano by offering him a good home."

"Kano!" I cried. Nona's last husband, the artist, had a gentle black dog who followed him everywhere.

"You remember him?"

I nodded. "I loved that dog. But I never knew he

belonged to anyone else. I nicknamed him Splatter because he'd wag his tail into my grandpa's paints and splatter paint all over his fur. Sometimes the paint got on me, too." I smiled fondly, then frowned as I recalled what came next. "Grandpa and Kano both died the same summer. Nona never remarried or got another dog. But that was like five years ago. Why didn't you come here sooner?"

"Nona didn't deserve my problems."

"She would have wanted to help."

"Back then I wasn't such a trusting person."

"And you are now?"

"Well ... not so much." He gave me a bitter smile.

"But you couldn't have been older than thirteen or fourteen. How did you make it on your own?"

"I was tall for my age, so it was easy to pass for older. I worked on ranches, leaving whenever anyone asked too many questions. For a while I stayed with these retired teachers who home-schooled me. They got me reading poetry and going to the library. They guessed I was underage and hinted about wanting to adopt me ..." His voice trailed off, his expression saddening.

"So why didn't you stay with them?"

"They couldn't afford to keep their ranch, so they moved to Arizona near their grandkids. I'd gotten soft staying in one place so long, so I moved on."

"Didn't you try to find out what happened to your uncle?"

"Sure. I searched online but there wasn't anything. I even let myself hope I wasn't a killer ... that my uncle survived." His blue eyes went cold. "Now I know."

There was a ripple of music from my cell phone.

I ignored it until the third ring. When I saw who was calling, I swore under my breath and shut off the power, shoving the phone back in my pocket.

"Who was it?" Dominic asked.

"No one important." I reached out for his hand and curled my fingers around his. "Dominic, please stay here. What about your horse-shoeing classes?"

"Doesn't matter now." He turned back to his suitcase.

"Running your own farrier business is your dream!" I argued, walking around so he'd have to face me. "You can't give it up now. And you can't give up on the people who love you, either. What about us? Don't you care?"

He stopped, a pair of faded jeans hanging from his hand. "I care ... too much."

"Then stay, and we'll deal with this together. So what if a PI showed up looking for you? Didn't you hear Penny-Love? She told him he had the wrong person and sent him away. He's long gone by now."

"PIs don't give up that easily. And I need to be free—like Dagger." He gestured toward the bird, who'd settled on the wood perch by the high open window. "Jail would be a slow death. I'm sorry, Sabine. There's no other way."

"Please, Dominic." I fought the urge to cry.

His gaze swept around the room, at wall paintings, bookshelves, photos framed on his dresser, candles, incense, and a glass bowl of crystals, as if this would be his last look. Frowning, he slammed his suitcase shut. "I'll only take what I can carry."

Dominic was too damned proud to stay for his own sake. He didn't believe he deserved to be happy and had the stupid idea that leaving would protect me and Nona from his troubles. I'd have to try a different angle: hit hard and drastic.

"Dominic, were you lying to Mrs. DeMarco?" I demanded.

His suitcase slipped from his fingers to the floor with a startling thump. "What are you talking about?"

"Don't you remember your promise to help Horse?" I folded my arms across my chest and pierced him with a steely look. "If you leave now, you'll break your promise."

"I'm no help to anyone now."

"Then Horse will die."

I wasn't playing fair, but I was desperate. I was counting on his stubborn sense of honor. If I could just make him stay longer—at least until Nona returned—we could find a solution that did *not* include Dominic leaving.

But Nona wasn't due back until tonight.

I could tell by Dominic's expression, shifting from determination to doubt, that my accusation had cut to his heart. I felt guilty for manipulating him like this ... but also hopeful, because it was working.

When he stepped away from the suitcase and sank down on the corner of the bed, I came to sit beside him. I placed my hand on his arm. "You'll stay?"

His shoulders slumped, defeated. "I honestly don't know."

"Well, I do," I said, with much more confidence than I felt. "And I know Nona will feel the same way. If the PI shows up again, we'll cover for you and find out the whole situation. Maybe he only wants to ask you questions. He might not even suspect you of your uncle's death."

"He didn't track me down after five years just for a few questions."

"Well, he can't do anything if he can't find you. Nona and I will hide you."

"And risk arrest for harboring a fugitive? Forget it."

"Too late," I said stubbornly. "You're stuck with us."

He said nothing for a moment, picking up a green crystal and rolling it between his callused fingers. His expression was dark, lost in thoughts. "I don't break promises," he finally said. "I'll try to help Josh and Horse. Then I'll handle things on my own. Okay?"

No, it wasn't okay. But it was the best I could hope for right now. So I agreed.

"I'll move my truck out of sight and then get on with my chores. There's a gate latch that needs fixing." He glanced toward the pasture. "You better go talk to Penny-Love."

"I'd rather stay with you."

"You want her to come looking for you?" he asked with a wry smile.

"She would, too. Promise you won't go anywhere?"

He nodded, but it was a temporary kind of nod.

I reached for him, and murmuring my name, he opened his arms and I folded into his embrace. So close, so warm, so hard to believe this could all end. I pressed my cheek against his chest, hearing the quick thumping of his heart. I'd hold tight to him and never let go. What we had was real and deep, and I knew he felt the same way.

He loved me. But that wouldn't stop him from leaving.

6

My world had cracked, splintering into brittle pieces. As I walked back to the farmhouse, my feet sloshing on the same path I'd taken a zillion times, everything around me looked different. The cloudy sky seemed darker, too, boiling with angry clouds and whipping out a biting cold wind that pierced my skin.

Dominic wanted to be with me and I wanted to be with him—wasn't that enough? Why did that horrible PI have to show up? Dominic hadn't meant to kill his uncle.

But could he prove it? Running away and changing his name would look suspicious. He'd need a good lawyer, and fortunately my father just happened to be one. But how could I convince Dominic to hire Dad?

Sunk in despair, the last thing I wanted to do was to listen to Penny-Love about who was dating/cheating/lying/playing someone else at school. But she had no idea I was going through a crisis and there wasn't anything I could do for Dominic, at least not until Nona came home.

When I entered the farmhouse, a cocoon of comfort blanketed me. I didn't exactly feel better, but I was less anxious. The living room was full of familiar friends—a collage of framed photos over the TV, a blue-gold afghan Nona crocheted for me, and the wooden coffee table that I'd carved my initials into when learning my ABCs.

The air smelled comforting, too—vanilla cinnamon tea—and I followed the sweet scent to the kitchen, where I found Penny-Love at the table. Her eyes were puffy and red as if she'd been crying.

So I poured myself a cup of tea, then pulled up a chair beside her. I slipped my arm around her shoulders and asked her to tell me what had happened.

"My life is over. Jacques dumped me."

Her hurt cut through me, and I could feel her pain—I was close to losing the guy I loved, too.

"Oh, Pen! He's a jerk and doesn't deserve you."

"He didn't even tell me in person. He texted me."

"That's brutal! No wonder you're so sad."

"Sad? More like furious." She thumped her fist on the table, drops of tea sloshing from her cup. "This is not the way things are supposed to go. I'm the one who does the breaking up, but he beat me to it."

"Excuse me?" I reached for a napkin and wiped the spilled tea. "You mean you were going to break up with *him?*"

"Not until after New Year's. He hardly ever calls and we don't have much in common." She paused to sip her tea. "Do you have any idea how humiliating it is to get dumped right before Christmas?"

"Josh dumped me after Thanksgiving."

"Not the same thing. You immediately hooked up with Dominic. I don't have a new guy lined up. The girls on the squad will pity me—which is just wrong."

I tried to follow her logic but felt like I'd taken the wrong turn in a maze. "I'm sorry," was all I could say.

"Sorry! Don't you get it?" She glared at me. "Being the rejected object of pity is ego-damaging. I hear my brothers talk all the time about ex-girlfriends, and I've vowed never to be the dumpee."

"Sometimes it just happens," I said sympathetically.

"Not to me. That's why I have a plan."

"Put a hit out on Jacques?"

"As if there's time for that." She shook her fiery curls like I'd been serious. "I need him alive and by my side for the Booster Club New Year's Party."

"You still want to date him?"

"Only till New Year's. Then, if he still wants to end it, fine. See, I have this theory that Jacques text-dumped me because he knew if he saw me in person, he'd want to be with me. I'm not bragging, it's just a fact. I have an unusual amount of guy magnetism."

I tried not to smile.

"I've decided to forgive Jacques and offer him a second chance."

"You think he'll agree?" I asked doubtfully. Penny-Love's concept of romance could be a little unrealistic.

"Abso-posi-lutely." She flashed me a confident grin. "The only hitch is I don't know where Jacques lives."

"You've been dating the guy over a month and haven't seen his house?"

"He says a gentleman always picks a lady up at her home. I thought it was so old-world and sweet, I never thought to ask about his place. He mentioned living in an apartment on the west side. I'll search online, then surprise him by going over."

I was about to point out what a bad idea this was when I heard a car coming down our driveway. I knew, from the unique rumble, that it was Thorn driving up in her mom's yellow VW bug.

Thorn and Penny-Love in the same room?

If Penny-Love was a whirlwind of drama, Thorn was a volatile black hole.

On the surface, my friends were complete opposites but stereotypical: Popularity-Plus Penny-Love and Rebel-Outsider Thorn. Yet I knew them better, and I liked them both. Penny-Love strived for perfection and popularity, embracing trendy fashions, but she mixed and matched things to suit herself. Thorn was anti-trends and anti-popularity, seeking independence from rules and society, but she was there for me in a crunch. And when it came to going after what they wanted, my friends were equally fearless.

When Penny-Love saw Thorn getting out of the VW, she took it better than I'd expected, merely lecturing me on how bad it was for my reputation to hang out with a "Goth freak."

"Didn't you say you had work to do in Nona's office?" I asked tactfully.

"I get the hint. And while I'm working, I'll Google Jacques to find his address." She refilled her tea cup before heading down the hall. "But if I come back and find you wearing black leather or planning on getting your nose pierced, I'm not going to be happy."

"No piercings," I promised, smiling.

Minutes later, there was a knock on the door.

Thorn looked almost ordinary today, having replaced her usual black leather and combat boots with white sneakers and black jeans. It wasn't until she brushed past me that I saw the barbed wire woven into her braids, the tiny rhinestones on her eyelids, and the dagger eyebrow-piercing.

"Thanks for coming over so quickly," I told her as she took the chair in the kitchen that Penny-Love had just vacated. I stood up and went to heat the tea water, remembering Thorn's preferred herbal flavor.

"I wasn't doing anything better. Everyone else at my house was headed for church."

"Well, your mother *is* a minister."

"She practices her sermons over and over till I could give them myself." Thorn rolled her eyes. "So what's up?"

I quickly filled her in on the Josh situation.

"Impressive," Thorn said when I was finished. "I didn't think a prep like him would have the guts to cut school."

"He didn't cut—he's missing and in danger."

"And you know this *how?*" she asked, with a doubtful twist of her black-lined lips.

I hesitated, always embarrassed to talk about my visions. But Thorn wasn't a stranger to psychic abilities and I knew she'd understand. So I described the strange place and cloaked people I'd seen in my vision. I shuddered when I told her about the knife.

"Intenseness." The dagger in her pierced brow rose slightly as she studied me. "Still ... I'm gonna pass."

I hadn't expected her to say "yes" immediately, but her quick refusal was disappointing. "Come on, Thorn. I'm not asking much. I just want you to touch something of Josh's."

"Do I look like a performing circus animal?"

"I never said you were."

"I don't have any real skill, not like your visions or how Dominic communicates with animals."

"Sure you do. You're a Finder, and I need your help to find Josh."

"Why the obsession with Josh?" Thorn idly twisted the barbed-wire bracelet on her wrist. "He was so not right for you. Get over him."

"I am over him," I insisted.

"Then forget about finding him."

"It's his family and his dog who need him to come home," I pointed out. And if I hadn't hurt him so badly, he wouldn't have left in the first place.

"Josh is almost an adult. He can go where he wants."

"But his life could be in danger."

"Since when did you get so overdramatic?"

I frowned. "I have this gut feeling that if I don't find him soon, he may never come back. I wouldn't ask for your help if I wasn't really worried."

"Like I can do anything—not."

"I'm only asking you to try. Come on, Thorn. It'll be interesting."

She glared at me, then relaxed with a sigh. "Why do I let you talk me into these things? You're getting to be as big a pain in the butt as Manny. So let's get this done already. What do you want me to touch?"

I pulled out the wand. "This belongs to Josh."

"How did you get it?"

Heat rushed to my cheeks. "I sort of took it from his room."

"Stealing?" She chuckled. "You naughty girl."

"I borrowed it. I'm going to return it."

"Why waste your time? It's cheap junk from a dollar store. Are you sure it belonged to Josh?"

"You tell me. Touch it."

She sipped her tea, then pushed the cup aside and grasped the wand. As her fingers settled over the smooth plastic, the energy in the room changed; the small hairs on my skin shivered.

Thorn's eyes closed, and a complete serenity settled over her soft features. Her aura changed, too, softening into pastels of pink and yellow. Without her prickly attitude vibes, she looked surprisingly vulnerable and pretty.

The rooster-shaped clock over the fridge ticked on, slowly.

Thorn's glittery lashes fluttered open and she sat the wand down on the table. "Map. Now."

I jumped up. After digging through three desk drawers, I finally found a road map of California. I rushed back to give it to Thorn.

She had a glazed look, as if part of her was still somewhere else—a feeling I knew too well from my own psychic experiences. If I closed my eyes and focused, would I slip into her world, leaving this body at home?

I didn't try to find out, just tapped my foot while Thorn unfolded the map, spreading it across the table. She waved her arms, swaying oddly, and looked up rather than down. Then she reached out with her hand, her finger pointing as it aimed and landed on the map.

"Here," she said.

I leaned over and saw her black-painted fingernail pointing to a dark green area of National Forest east of Auburn.

"That's a large area. Can you pinpoint a town?"

Thorn shook her head, blinking as she came back to reality. "I don't really know ... somewhere close to where I pointed, give or take a hundred miles." She brushed her fingers across the crystal star on the wand. "Weird thing is at first I wasn't picking up any male energy—only female. Very strong female energy."

I remembered the vision of the copper-haired woman I'd picked up from the wand. "A woman gave it to Josh, I think. I don't know who."

Thorn handed the wand back to me. "I got nothing else."

"Can't you try again?"

"I do what I can do, no promises."

Frustrated, I stared at the map. "But that's like a hundred miles of wilderness. I didn't learn enough to start a search for Josh."

"But I learned plenty," someone interrupted.

There was Penny-Love standing in the doorway, grinning.

Thorn glared at me. "Sabine, why didn't you tell me *she* was here!"

"Obviously Sabine is very good at keeping secrets," Penny-Love said accusingly.

"I'm sorry, Thorn," I said, the room now ridiculous with energy—and not the good kind. "I didn't know she was listening. Pen, how could you?"

"It wasn't easy. I couldn't hear much until I cracked the door open. Then I heard enough to know that you can help me." Penny-Love pointed to Thorn.

"Me, help you?" Thorn scoffed. "You're delusional."

"I could be on the phone right now, texting the video I just took of you doing that weird Finding thing with the map to all of my friends. It could even end up on You-Tube. Freaky news spreads fast."

"You wouldn't dare."

"Oh, I would. But hey, I'll delete the whole thing if you do one little favor for me. Afterwards, we can return to our mutual relationship of dislike and avoidance."

Thorn glared at Penny-Love, then at me, then back at her.

"What favor?" she asked through gritted teeth.

"Take me to Jacques."

7

Penny-Love and Thorn reached a temporary alliance. Tomorrow after school, Thorn would work her "Finding Mojo," as Pen called it, to find Jacques. In return, Penny-Love vowed never to speak of Thorn's skill to anyone.

But could the Gossip Queen of Sheridan High keep a secret?

Doubtful. Still, their temporary truce was better than a knock-'em-down, hair-pulling, blood-spilling fight.

After their contract was signed, Thorn tucked it safely

into her pocket and went home. A short while later, Penny-Love left too, blaming family obligations. I felt restless. It was almost lunch time, but I was too anxious about Dominic to eat. I wasn't sure what to do. I'd planned to spend the day going all "shopoholic" with Penny-Love at the mall, and now all I could think about was Dominic. What was he doing right now? What if he'd left without telling me? I had to see him, make sure he was okay. I'd just grabbed my coat when I heard the roar of a car's engine.

"Nona!" I would have recognized the sound of her clunker car anywhere.

The door banged behind me as I hurried outside, almost crying with relief at the sight of my grandmother—and not only because I missed her. Since recovering from a serious illness, Nona was more energetic and sharper than ever. She'd know how to make Dominic stay.

Nona burst out of her car like a brisk wind, opening her arms to me. "There's my favorite girl!" She smelled of peppermint and peach shampoo.

I hugged her tight. "I'm so glad you're back!"

"It's good to be home," she said, stroking my hair lightly from my face.

"Wait till I tell you what's happened…" I started to say, at the same time that she exclaimed, "I have amazing news to tell you!"

We both laughed, and I told her to go first.

"Well, you know I went to San Francisco for business,"

she said, lifting a suitcase from the car trunk. I reached out to help her. "And it turned out to be not just a business trip."

"What do you mean?" I asked, following her into the house.

Nona draped her knitted purple scarf across a worn leather chair. "I met a brilliant, witty, wonderful man." A blush softened her sun-wrinkled cheeks. "His name's Roger Aimsley, and he's the owner of Heart Lights, a very successful online dating service. Much higher profile than my little business. He surprised me with a proposal."

"Proposal? You're getting married again?" I groaned. Nona had been married too many times already, twice to the same man. This did *not* sound good.

"Not marriage, although who knows what the future will bring? This is about a different kind of union—one that will change my future."

Memo to self: no more weekend trips for Nona. "I don't understand," I said.

My grandmother shook out of her coat and draped it over the back of the rocking chair. Her green eyes sparkled and her hands moved as she went on excitedly, "I didn't answer him yet. I told him I needed to talk it over with you and Penny-Love."

"Why Pen?"

"She's part of my business now. Roger has offered me a partnership, combining our businesses."

I listened to her explain the many benefits of merging Soul-Mate Matches with Heart Lights. But she didn't want to rush into anything, she insisted, and planned to consult astrology charts and tarot cards before signing any papers. She was practically dancing as she talked, and sparkling in a way I hadn't seen in a long time. I hated to ruin her moment with my far-from-good news.

Still, it had to be done.

I gathered my thoughts, trying to come up with the easiest way to spring the bad news on her. Finally, I just spit it all out, starting with the phone call from Mrs. DeMarco this morning and finishing with the PI and Dominic. Her quick change of expression showed that she'd suspected Dominic's violent secret and grasped the seriousness of his situation.

"Dominic says he's leaving," I finished sadly.

"Rubbish!" She shook her silvery-brown head. "He doesn't mean it."

"Yes, he does! He thinks leaving is the way to stay out of jail and protect us from any trouble, too."

"That boy can be danged mule-headed."

"Tell me about it." I sighed. "How can we help him if he won't let us?"

"Call in the troops."

"Troops?"

"My angel cards and spirit guides." Nona squeezed my

hand gently. "Don't worry, Sabine. Dominic isn't going anywhere."

She sounded so positive. I wanted to believe her, but my gut feeling tightened like a noose and all I could taste was fear.

*   *   *

A half hour later, Nona headed to the barn to talk to Dominic. She didn't invite me to come along. Instead, she told me to stay close to the phones in case she got an important call. From the way she said "important," I guessed she meant Roger Aimsley (or, as I'd mentally nick-named him, Mr. Heart Lights).

He didn't call, but my cell went off four times—and when I checked Caller ID I nearly threw the phone down. *Jade again.* Why did she keep calling? She'd shown she didn't want to be my friend or my sister. I definitely did *not* want to talk to her.

I deleted her messages.

Retreating to my room, I sought inner calm by burning incense and pulling my latest embroidery project from my craft bag. Several of my Christmas gifts would be handmade. I'd already personalized pillow cases in shimmering hues for my parents and was almost finished with a set for Nona. For my twin sisters, I strung tiny alphabet letter beads into dainty ankle bracelets. Amy and Ashley appreciated our tradition of homemade gifts—it was much better than gift certificates or random items that usually needed to be exchanged.

I already had two perfectly good sisters.

I did *not* need another one.

I stabbed the needle into my finger three times before shoving it all back into my craft bag. Crossing the room to the attic window, which offered an amazing view of Nona's farm, I pressed my face against the glass and peered down at the barn. Would Dominic still be here for Christmas? Was he inside with Nona right now? What were they saying?

I turned from the window. Stressing over Dominic was only making me crazy. I needed to keep busy, to distract myself. Jumbled wrapping paper, boxes, and bags were spread across my bed. There were only a few names left on my Christmas list. After crossing Jade's name out with heavy black "hate you forever" lines, I decided to do something extra special for my *real* sisters.

At ten years old, Amy and Ashley already had such distinct personalities that people couldn't tell at first glance that they were identical twins. Glamtastic Ashley sparkled in her style and musicality. She wrote songs and loved discovering new talent to add to her playlists. So it only took me a few minutes to go online and order songs from a new R&B artist for her.

But book butterfly (not bookworm!) Amy's biggest passion was collecting vintage girl-series books like Nancy Drew and Judy Bolton mysteries. Her collection was getting so large it was hard to find something she didn't already have. I surfed online sites and got lucky, finding a rare book—*All About Collecting Girls' Series Books*—by John Axe. As I clicked "buy" online, my IM flashed an incoming message.

It was Jade. Again. What was her problem? She'd made it clear she couldn't stand me. Why couldn't she just let things drop?

The message box popped on my screen:

Wkg on prob. Need 2 talk. Urgent!

"I have enough problems of my own, thank you very much," I murmured sarcastically. "Not interested in yours."

I deleted the message.

As I returned to surfing online, I kept expecting another message from Jade. But there weren't any, which was good, I assured myself. As Dominic said, just because we were sisters didn't make us friends.

I'd hoped to get Dominic's thoughts on Jade at dinner, but he didn't show up. I nearly stormed out to his loft to force him to talk to me. But Nona warned me to give him space, that he needed time to think. Although Nona didn't seem worried, I lay awake long into the night with a deep gut fear that I'd wake up tomorrow and find Dominic gone.

I finally sank into a sound sleep, and it was so deep that I slept in late and had to rush getting ready for school. I'd only taken a few bites of muffin when a car honked from outside. Chewing fast, I grabbed my backpack and almost flew down the steps.

But I stopped at the sound of a horse's whinny and peered off into the pasture, to see Dominic brushing down Rio. Thank god he was still here! He turned and looked right at me, lifting his arm to wave. I lifted my arm, too. I couldn't see his expression, but I knew our wave was like a promise. When I returned home from school, Dominic would be waiting. For me.

Smiling, I hurried into Penny-Love's car.

Penny-Love was wearing all black: snug black jeans, a black aviator jacket over a lacy midnight-black blouse, and an onyx beaded bracelet. Her curly red hair was pulled back severely in a braid and even though the sun wasn't out, she wore dark sunglasses.

"Do you like my spy look?"

"So that's what the black is about," I said with a wry smile. "I thought Thorn's Goth style had rubbed off on you."

"Oh, puh-leese! Like that would ever happen! But since Thorn and I are going to find Jacques later, I didn't want anyone to recognize me."

"Embarrassed about being seen with Thorn?"

"Don't be ridiculous." She touched her burgundy-painted nails to her chest in mock indignation. "We may have to follow Jacques, you know, like in action movies. This is my incognito look. You, on the other hand, look like crap. Some makeup would fix your puffy eyes. Are you sick or something?"

"Good morning to you, too. If you must know, I had trouble sleeping."

"Too bad." She nodded absent-mindedly as she slowed for a stop sign. Her gaze drifted off to ogle a group of guys cruising by. Knowing Pen, she was already lining up someone to take Jacques' place.

By the time we reached school, Pen had spilled all the latest gossip: a football player caught his mom making out with his coach; some kids were busted for dealing drugs on campus; and cheerleading friends Kaitlyn and Catelyn were feuding... again.

It was surreal to be sitting in class, half-listening to teachers and trying to manage ordinary conversation when all I could think about was Dominic. I found myself floating out of my own body, the conscious part of me hovering ghostlike over my physical self. It was calming to rise above it all, detached, without any real emotions. I watched myself, surprised that the blond girl could smile and talk so casually with friends like the world wasn't slipping off its axis. Penny-Love was right about my puffy eyes, but otherwise you'd never know anything was wrong.

Sabine Rose performed her school role very well.

At lunch break I moved on autopilot, heading as usual to the computer room, which had become my retreat since breaking up with Josh. As I crossed a busy hall intersection, bodies rushing all directions, I nearly ran into Manny DeVries handing out flyers.

Manny looked wickedly hot as usual, a cross between a pirate and a surfer with his sleek black dreads, pierced eyebrow, and leather sandals. Rain or icy chill, Manny always wore his trademark sandals. He was the editor of our school newspaper, the *Sheridan Shout-Out*, and I worked as his copyeditor.

"Hey, Beany!" he called to me.

I cringed at the nickname. Would he ever learn to say my actual name?

"What are you doing?" I asked, eyeing the thick stacks of paper he was carrying.

"Spreading my news," he said with a devilish grin. "Take a bunch and pass them out."

"Sorry, not now." I started to walk past, but he'd already shoved papers into my hands. And since few people had the fortitude to refuse Manny, I gave in and started helping him.

When I'd started at Sheridan High this fall, my plan was to fit in without standing out, and aim for mid-popularity status. I'd joined the newspaper staff as a way to keep in touch behind the scenes and found a friend in Manny DeVries—a handsome, dark-skinned guy with wild dreads and an outspoken, brazen attitude. Despite our differences, or maybe because of them, we worked well together. I was quiet; he was loud. I was polite; he was bossy and rude.

I avoided crowds; his charismatic personality drew crowds like fans flocking to a rock star.

"So what is this anyway?" I asked, shoving papers at random passers-by.

"A flyer announcing a special issue of the *Sheridan Shout-Out*," Manny said proudly.

"What special issue?"

"The one I've decided to put out on Friday—the last day before winter vacation—as the newspaper's staff gift to our loyal readers. It's going to have special interviews, amazing gift coupons, and bonus predictions from Mystic Manny."

He might have been Mystic Manny, but his predictions were all mine. The secret arrangement benefited us both—Manny helped me whenever I needed hacker skills, and I gave him astonishingly true predictions.

"I hadn't planned to spend my lunch this way," I told him.

"Fun things just happen when I'm around," he joked.

"Your idea of fun isn't mine."

He chuckled, and then flashed a flirty smile at a brunette with pretty dark eyes and a very low-cut blouse. "Just pass out the papers. Then I'll tell you all about your big assignment for Mystic Manny. You're gonna love it."

I shook my head, but kept up a polite smile as I handed out papers.

"Come on, Beany, you know you'll end up doing

what I want, so let's just skip the arguments. Pretend I've already spent a day begging for your help and you gave in because that's just the kind of sweet person you are." He gave me that cocky grin that won some girls' hearts. But not mine. I had Dominic... but for how long?

"Fine. Whatever." I didn't have the energy to battle today. "What does Mystic Manny need from me?"

"Nothing much... just a few extra Ten Years in the Future predictions."

This feature was Mystic Manny's most popular—a random student was given a prediction of what his/her life would be in ten years. Last week I'd predicted that Carrie Marquez, a junior on the track team, would invent a gadget which would make her rich.

"How many more predictions?" I raised my eyebrows. "Two or three?"

"Twelve."

"TWELVE!"

"It's a Twelve Days of Christmas theme."

"Forget it. It'll take weeks of meditation to come up with that many!"

"I need it by Thursday."

Three days? He had to be kidding. I looked at him, waiting for the chuckle at his joke, but his black eyes met mine with seriousness. I didn't even bother to argue. There was no winning with Manny. But I didn't give in either, and with an exasperated "Humph!" strode past him into the computer room. I pulled out my sack lunch and ate while playing mindless computer games.

During sixth period Manny didn't bring up the subject again, and when the final bell rang, I was so out of there. Every minute away from Dominic was torture, and all I could think about was being with him. So when Penny-Love offered me a ride home, I jumped at the chance to see Dominic sooner.

When I saw Thorn sitting in the front seat next to Pen, it was weird. Like looking at one of those puzzles where you're supposed to match things that belong together.

Thorn and Pen definitely did *not* belong together.

"Where are you two headed?" I asked, slipping into the back seat and clicking my seat belt.

"Jacque's apartment," Penny-Love answered as she started the engine.

"So you found out where he lives?" I asked.

"Thorn did her Finding magic."

"I told you, it's not magic." Thorn gave a long suffering sigh. "I just looked at a city map and kind of saw an apartment and address. Although not the exact apartment."

"But that won't be hard to figure out once we get there," Penny-Love finished.

"Well, thanks for dropping me off," I told them.

"Actually..." Penny-Love caught my gaze in the rearview mirror. "Actually, we're not dropping you off."

"What!" I exclaimed. "Why not?"

"Thorn and I need you around to prevent us from killing each other. So we agreed you should come with us."

"Well, I didn't agree. Take me home right now."

"Too late. We just passed your road," Penny-Love said without an ounce of regret in her tone. "Guess you're coming with us."

8

Short of jumping out of the moving car, what could I do?
They were my friends. I guessed it wouldn't kill me to go
with them—except every mile took me further away from
Dominic.

Do not resist the unexpected journey, my spirit guide
advised in my head.

"Opal?" I closed my eyes so I could see her clearly…
queenly black hair coiled on her head like a crown, high
cheekbones, wise ebony eyes.

You're uneasy, which is understandable, but you would do well to conserve your energy for the road ahead, when your choices will influence those close to you who balance precariously between life and death.

Whatever that meant, it couldn't be good. I was already on a road I hadn't chosen, with my two closest friends—was one of them in danger? I bit my lip, glancing at Penny-Love and Thorn in the front seat of the car. Thorn was criticizing Penny-Love for making such a sharp turn out of the school parking lot that she nearly ran down a kid lugging a tuba case.

"Is there something I should know?" I wordlessly asked my spirit guide.

Knowledge would deter the natural course with cumbersome negative emotions. You continue to be the nucleus of events which will bond or break those you hold dear to your heart. Your challenges are the stepping stones upon which others will tread during their climb to enlightenment.

"Huh?" I thought back.

You'll understand in time, but when the moment of choice comes, your decisions will either open doors for a loved one or slam them shut forever.

"Is this about Dominic? Is he in danger?"

I can't answer that without influencing your choices. Remember, heed your heart and act from love not anger.

She faded before I could ask anything else—an annoying habit.

I tried to decipher Opal's message. She'd been warning me about Dominic, I figured, and the mention of shutting doors hinted that Dominic was going to leave if I couldn't help him. I needed to talk to him—before it was too late.

When I pulled out my cell phone, Thorn twisted around in her seat to look at me. "Calling the cops on us?" she asked, the corners of her black-shimmered lips curving with wry humor.

"I should."

"And what would you say?" Thorn chuckled darkly. "'Officer, I'm being held captive by a dangerous Goth chick and her cheerleader accomplice.'"

"Accomplice?" Penny-Love snorted. "Taking Sabine was my idea."

"I'll be sure to tell that to the cops when they come to arrest us," Thorn said.

"No one is getting arrested," Penny-Love said, catching my gaze in the rear view mirror. "Sabine won't admit it, but she'd rather be with us than anyone else."

"I'd rather be with my boyfriend," I insisted, waving my cell phone.

"Can't blame you." Pen wolf-whistled. "Dominic is hotter than a heat wave, you lucky girl."

Not so lucky if Dominic leaves, I thought anxiously with a glance at the illuminated clock on the car's dashboard. Precious seconds I could be with Dominic flashed by, and the phone kept ringing, unanswered. "Damn. He's not picking up."

"Don't stress," Penny-Love suggested. "He'll call back."

He might … or maybe not. Getting a better idea, I called my grandmother.

"Oh … Sabine."

Was that disappointment I heard in Nona's voice? But there was no time to quiz her about who she'd hoped was calling (a certain Mr. Heart Lights?). Quickly, I explained that I was with friends and would be home later. When I asked about Dominic, she said he'd gone to talk to the instructor at his horse-shoeing school. Was he dropping out?

As I snapped my phone closed, Thorn asked softly, "Things okay with you and Dominic?"

"Never better." I summoned a smile. "We're doing great."

Thorn studied me. "Then why do you seem uptight?"

"I was hoping to be with him by now. Not here."

"This shouldn't take long," she assured me.

"Going with me is not torture," Penny-Love interrupted. "You see Dominic every day, but how often do you get the chance to watch the drama of a romantic reunion?"

"Romantic?" Thorn snorted, the map spread across her lap slipping down her knees so she had to grab for it. "You wish."

"Hey, it'll be reality-show worthy. When I show up at Jacques' apartment, he won't be able to resist me and he'll beg me to come back."

"What planet were you raised on?" Thorn asked. "Guys don't work like that."

"Jacques isn't boring and childish like most high school guys. He's exciting and mature."

"Mature means too old for you," Thorn said.

I nodded, agreeing with Thorn. The few times I'd been around Jacques I'd had an odd feeling, like something was out of balance. He *did* seem older and I'd heard rumors he was into drugs, although Penny-Love refused to listen to anything negative about him. He'd seemed okay enough—at least until he dumped my best friend.

"He's eighteen," Penny-Love told Thorn. "I prefer older men."

"He's that for sure." Thorn tapped her black-painted fingernails on the arm rest. "Did he get held back or flunk?"

"He did not flunk—he's an A student and a senior. Who cares if he got held back twice? That's only part of why he's so mature. And what do you know about guys anyway?" Penny-Love's voice rose in anger. "You don't even date."

"I've dated," Thorn argued. "I'm just not into anyone right now."

"Or like, ever. What about the geeky guy who follows you around."

"Who? You can't mean KC?" Thorn shook her dark, pink-streaked head.

"Yeah, average looking and all around forgettable.

And he's always following you around at school. Didn't he used to be homeless?"

"So what if he was? He's living with my family now."

"Sharing your room?" Penny-Love kept one hand on the wheel as she turned to wink at Thorn.

"Not even!" Thorn glared. "He's sharing with my brothers, and he is definitely not into me. I mean, he's like another brother."

"The way he looks at you isn't brotherly," Penny-Love said, and she'd know because she didn't miss much of what went on at school.

"Keep talking stupid and I'll shove this map down your throat," Thorn warned.

Penny-Love only laughed. "Oh, I'm scared!"

"If you weren't driving, you'd be dead already."

"And if you weren't-"

"ENOUGH!" I screamed, straining my seat belt and spreading my arms between them. They weren't kidding about needing a referee. "Let's focus on the goal here. Finding Jacques, remember?"

"But what she said—"

I stopped Penny-Love with a scathing look.

"Fine, fine." She backed down. "I don't care what she thinks anyway. After Jacques is mine again, I won't get five feet near the Goth pit of losers at school."

"And I'll avoid pathetic cheerleader clones."

Penny-Love started to retort, then suddenly pointed to a street sign. "Thorn, isn't that where we turn?"

Thorn quickly consulted the map. "Yeah."

"Right or left?" Penny-Love asked.

"Right." Thorn made a gesture toward the window. "Then go about a mile and make another right."

"This can't be the way." Penny-Love said, biting her lower lip as she glanced around at the businesses with barred windows. "Jacques wouldn't live in such a yucky area."

"You expected a mansion?" Thorn asked.

"No, but something better than this. Maybe a nice condo, you know, in the suburbs."

"Not everyone can afford a house," I pointed out. "Maybe his parents don't have a lot of money or lost their jobs."

She shook her head. "Jacques doesn't live with his parents. He lives with an older brother who's a phlebotomist."

"A fleb-what?" I asked.

"A blood sucker." Penny-Love laughed. "Drawing blood at a hospital. And Jacques does some construction work on weekends, so he's got plenty of cash—once I saw a bunch of hundreds in his wallet. I figured he'd live somewhere nice."

"Not so nice," Thorn put in as she pointed to a faded, puke-colored, three-story apartment complex called Gable Lombard Apartments.

Penny-Love groaned, swerving to avoid a hole in the pavement and jerking me backwards. "Thorn, your Finding radar is wrong."

"Not wrong." Thorn waved the folded map. "He's

here all right. I can feel the energy stronger, coming from somewhere over there."

"The first floor?" I guessed, following her pointing finger. "So that narrows it down to about a dozen apartments. How are you going to find the right one?"

"If he's here, we'll find him." Penny-Love pulled over and shut off the engine.

"Keep me out of this," I told her. "You made me come along, but I'm not going any farther than this car. I want to try calling Dominic again. Good luck finding Jacques."

And no matter how much she whined, I refused to leave the car. I was relieved that Thorn didn't push me. She simply stepped out of the car and started for the apartment. Penny-Love gave me one last exasperated look, then hurried after Thorn.

I watched my two mismatched friends walk up a cracked sidewalk into the apartment complex. Was it a good idea leaving them on their own? Could they get along five minutes without killing each other? For a moment I had my hand on the door handle, ready to go after them. But then I dropped my hand and reached for my phone.

I listened to five rings until Dominic's recorded voice invited me to leave a message.

"It's me," I said. "Talk to you later."

Clicking off, I gave a deep sigh of frustration, worry, and loneliness. I was sure Dominic hadn't left…yet. He wouldn't until he'd helped Josh and Horse, and since Josh still wasn't at school, I guessed he was still missing. And I was definitely worried about Dominic.

I tried to imagine what he was doing right now and closed my eyes, willing a vision. Nothing came, as if the connection I usually felt with Dominic was blocked by a wall. He was shutting me out. Was it intentional? Was he pulling away from me so that when he left for good, I couldn't find him?

I don't know how long I stared out the window thinking about Dominic, but suddenly I heard someone shouting my name. Jerking up so quickly that I bumped my elbow on the door, I saw Thorn dragging Penny-Love to the car, their auras a firestorm of blazing reds.

"Hurry, hurry!" Thorn flung open the passenger door and shoved Penny-Love into the front seat.

"Is something wrong?" I asked.

"Buckle up!" she ordered without stopping to answer my question. She hurried to the driver's side and jumped in, keys jangling from her fingers.

"What's going on?" I clasped the front seat for balance when the car jerked to a start.

"We're getting out of here!" Thorn revved the engine.

"But why the urgency? And why are you driving?"

"Someone has to. She can't." Thorn thumbed at Penny-Love, her tone angry but a little scared, too.

Penny-Love said nothing as she fastened her seat belt. Her freckles stood out on her eerily pale face and her eyes stared ahead blankly. A reddish stain splattered her blouse sleeve. Dark red ... like blood.

"What happened?" I demanded again, worried.

Thorn, driving, shook her head. "Ask her. We have to get far away and fast."

"Pen, talk to me," I said. "Tell me what's going on."

But Penny-Love just stared ahead, blank, as if someone had hit the delete key on her personality. The only hint of emotion was a single tear sliding down her cheek.

"She hasn't said a word since it happened." Thorn yanked the wheel, jerking the car (and us) sideways.

"Since what ... Thorn!" I cried as she nearly collided with a garbage truck. "Slow down! Are you trying to kill us?"

"Kill us?" Thorn started to laugh, a bitter sound that scared me.

"Thorn, what's going on? And what did you do to Pen?"

"Me? You think I did something?" Thorn snarled. "She's the one who got us into this mess."

I turned back to Penny-Love, who still stared ahead with a vacant zombie expression. I turned her toward me, and my gaze connected with Penny-Love's blank stare. I felt myself jerked forward—and this time it had nothing to do with Thorn's wild driving. A searing wave of energy erupted and smothered me with startling intensity. Everything went dizzy as I lifted and spun, spun, spun ...

When the spinning stopped, I was still in the car, but at a different moment in time. I'd somehow time-traveled back to the moment when Thorn, Penny-Love, and I had arrived at the apartment. Only instead of staying in the car, I was moving across a parking lot and entering the building. And Thorn moved beside me, which confused me until I realized I wasn't replaying this moment as myself. My soul had hitched a ride on Penny-Love's memories.

We hesitated in a hallway until Thorn closed her eyes, trancelike, and pointed to the right. We walked down the narrow corridor on a stained carpet … faded orange paint and smells of cat pee, tacos, and mildew … Thorn was nodding as we approached the end of the hall.

"This is how it's going down," Penny-Love told Thorn as they passed Apartment 12. "I'll go inside alone. You wait in the hall while I work my charm on Jacques."

"Five minutes," Thorn snapped, clearly annoyed at being given orders. "If you're not back, I'm leaving."

I felt Penny-Love's face curve into a confident smile, everything about her upbeat and confident. She applied strawberry lip gloss and finger-combed her curly hair. As she lifted her arm to knock on the door of Apartment 18, she gave a soft cry of surprise. "It's already open!"

"That's weird," Thorn said, frowning.

"No, it's wonderful!" Penny-Love rejoiced. "It's a sign I'm meant to be here!"

"You're being stupid."

"You know your problem, Thorn? You have no sense of romance."

"And you know your problem, Cheerleader? You're—"

Before Thorn could tell her, Penny-Love gave a perky wave and sailed like a cool breeze into the apartment. "Jacques, I'm here," she called out as she raced through the living room, then down a hall where another door stood open like an invitation, as if he was expecting her.

She burst into the room ... then everything went blurry with violent colors of red and black. Something on the floor ... no, *someone.*

Penny-Love cried out, kneeling by the still body. Jacques ... Jacques ... why didn't he move? Lifting a limp arm and clasping his hand, begging him to move ... something sticky. She pulled back her hand, staring, horrified, at something wet on her fingers.

Sticky, damp, red ... blood.

And she screamed.

9

Energy whiplashed me back to the present, and the world went silent.

Thorn jerked the car to a bone-snapping stop.

I glanced out the window. We were now in a parking lot with no other cars, at the side of a large boxy building with a steeple spiraling from the roof toward heaven. *First Church of Sheridan Valley*, I read on a back-lit marquee.

"We can talk here," Thorn explained, unsnapping her seat belt and turning around.

"Is this where your mom works?" I guessed.

"Yeah ... for now anyway." Thorn's crimson lips pressed tight, like this was a topic she didn't want to go into. "There's no prayer meeting or Bible study tonight, so it's private. We have to talk about serious stuff."

"Jacques' death," I said, so softly I almost didn't hear my own voice.

"How did you know?" Thorn asked then she shook her head without waiting for me to answer. "Cut that question. You always know things that you shouldn't."

"So what I saw was real?" I rubbed my head. I was used to talking to people *after* they'd died but dream-viewing the bloody body of someone from my school was horrific. "Jacques really is dead?"

"Very dead," Thorn said with an uneasy glance at Penny-Love, who still stared off blankly at nothing. "I followed Pen into the apartment but waited in the living room. I noticed some official-looking folders scattered on a table. A photo attached to one folder startled me and I was reaching for it when I heard Pen scream. I didn't get too close to the body, but no way could I miss all the blood on his chest. It was either suicide or he pissed someone off pretty bad."

"Thorn!" I gave her a nasty look. "Some sensitivity, please."

"It's not like he can hear us."

"Pen can."

But Penny-Love still wasn't talking, and when I turned to look at her, she was staring down at her trembling, red-splotched hands.

I turned back to Thorn, something odd she said coming back to me. "You mentioned a folder and a photo that startled you. Who was in the photo?"

She frowned, rubbing her pierced eyebrow. "This isn't a good time to answer that question."

"When will be? Things are already critical. Whatever you saw can't make things any worse."

"Don't count on that."

"What are you hinting at?" I demanded. "Just tell me."

"Fine. But you won't like it. I only got a quick look at the folder. It was labeled *Hughes, Greyson* in black ink and had some kind of an official stamp in the corner. Stapled to the front were two photos: one of a freaky-tall blond dude and the other … well … it was Josh."

I opened my mouth to insist that Thorn had to be mistaken, but stopped when I heard Penny-Love sob Jacques' name. I'd continue this with Thorn later—right now Penny-Love was more important.

I reached out, touching Penny-Love's shoulder. "Take it easy, Pen. You can't do anything for Jacques."

"Sabine?" Penny-Love blinked at me like an ice statue slowly thawing. "Do you know what happened?"

I nodded.

"I can't believe it ... He was just lying there ... not moving."

"I'm sorry," was all I could think of to say.

A tear trickled down Penny-Love's freckled cheek. "Jacques can't be ... gone. He is ... was ... so talented, such an amazing artist, and too young to ... ohmygod! It has to be a mistake ... he should be alive ..."

"But he's not," Thorn cut in impatiently. "And we're the lucky finders of his dead body. Thanks a lot, Cheerleader."

"Don't be cruel, Thorn," I snapped.

"I'm being realistic. We have some serious decisions to make."

"What decisions?" My brain seemed stuck on pause. "We can't do anything to help him now, except call 911. Or did you call already?"

"I was more interested in getting the hell out of there."

"You ran from a crime scene?" I'd watched enough TV shows to know this wasn't a good idea.

"You bet I did, and dragging the zombie cheerleader with me wasn't easy either. She wouldn't let go of the corpse's hand. I practically had to carry her out of there. Do either of you have any idea of the trouble we could be in? If the police questioned us, we'd have to explain how we found Jacques. Do you really think they'd believe my Finding ability makes me a human GPS?"

"We could say we knew his address," I argued.

"One lie leads to another and another, and they'd guess we were hiding something. It would have been insane to stick around."

"But it was wrong to leave." I shook my head. "Now what are we supposed to do? Make an anonymous 911 call or just drive off and pretend we don't know he's dead?"

"Driving off works for me," Thorn said.

"My poor, poor Jacques," Penny-Love murmured.

"It's not like *she* can make any decisions." Thorn gestured at Penny-Love, who was now gazing out the car window and murmuring "Jacques" over and over. "She'd be sweating under police questioning if I hadn't hauled her ass out of there. Look at her—blood on her clothes and arm. She could be a prime suspect since Jacques dumped her. There'll be evidence of all that on their cell phones. "

"Suspect?" I repeated.

"Duh." Thorn rolled her kohl-shadowed eyes. "Whoever finds a body always looks guilty, so they might suspect me and you as accomplices."

"But we didn't do anything wrong."

"Can we prove it?"

I'd grown up on Dad's stories about his cases, including horror stories about innocent people accused of crimes. "Justice is a luxury that few can afford," Dad had once told me. At the time I wasn't sure what he meant, but now I understood.

I looked at Penny-Love. "You okay?"

Penny-Love shook her head, red curls tangling around her pale face. "Poor Jacques…so much blood. Who would do that to him?"

Thorn scowled. "Let's hope the police don't think it's his scorned ex-girlfriend."

"Huh?" Penny-Love choked. "You mean *me?*"

"Just saying the police might jump to conclusions."

"Thorn, don't scare her," I said, reaching up to give Penny-Love's shoulder a reassuring pat. "She's gone through a horrible shock."

"She needs to get over it real fast. We have to get our stories straight or go through a nightmare of police drama. Fortunately we got out of there quickly without disturbing the crime scene. We left before I touched that folder. What about you, Cheerleader?" Thorn shifted in her seat to face Penny-Love. "Did you touch anything?"

Penny-Love didn't answer right away, her gaze still unfocused and her movements slow. "It's all hazy and hard to remember…I started to knock on the door only it was already open and I saw the TV on but no one was watching so I went down to the bedroom and that door was open, too…"

"So you didn't touch any doors," Thorn said with relief. "Neither did I. We didn't leave anything CSI types can trace back to us."

"Except maybe one thing," Penny-Love interrupted quietly.

"What?" Thorn demanded.

"I touched Jacques." Penny-Love rubbed the reddish spots on her hands. "I didn't know right away ... that he wasn't alive ... and I reached out to hold him."

"Blood will wash off," Thorn said. "Get rid of your clothes so there won't be anything to connect us to the crime scene."

Penny-Love nodded.

"I think our butts are covered." Thorn exhaled. "I don't think anyone saw us and we got out of there fast. If your fingerprints are on Jacques, who cares, you're his girlfriend. So we should be okay."

"Well ... except I did pick something up," Penny-Love confessed. "I didn't know what I was doing ... I never meant to touch it. But it fell from his hand when I reached for him, so I moved it."

"Moved what?" Thorn asked sharply.

"This."

I leaned so far over that my seat belt cut into my shoulder. I could see Penny-Love reach into her coat pocket and pull out a small, dark-gray gun.

Thorn swore.

My mouth gaped open.

All Penny-Love said was, "Oops."

10

Thorn smacked the steering wheel with such force that the car shook. Then she yelled at Penny-Love, "Put that thing away!"

Penny-Love did as she asked, then covered her face with her hands. She kept wailing, "I didn't mean to!" as her shoulders shook with sobs. My gaze fixated on the blood splatters on her arm, which somehow made the whole horrible situation even more horrible.

Thorn was furious, but to be honest, so was I. Find-

101

ing a dead body was bad enough. Bringing back what was probably the murder weapon was a zillion times worse. We were now tied to this crime. I hadn't even wanted to come with them, and now I could be arrested as an accomplice to murder. I should let Thorn and Penny-Love deal with this drama. But if I left them alone together they might add to the death toll by killing each other.

So I jumped in as referee again. After more tears and arguments, they calmed down. No one wanted to return the gun but no one wanted to keep it, either. Thorn wanted to bury it. Penny-Love wanted to toss it in a dumpster. My idea to anonymously mail the gun to the police was strongly out-voted.

Since no one could agree, Thorn said she'd hide the gun in a safe place until we could decide what to do. She wrapped it in napkins she found in the glove box, then left the car and went into a small building next to the church. About five minutes later she came out with empty hands.

Since I didn't want my psychic grandmother to get close enough to Thorn and Penny-Love to suspect that anything was wrong, I asked Thorn to drop me off on the street. As I walked the rest of the way home, I tried not to think of Jacques, cursing the vision that bound me to the crime. I wanted to wave a wand and be as innocent as a child.

And what about the folder Thorn saw? Why would Jacques have photos of Josh and Grey? This made absolutely no sense unless it had something to do with school—except Grey didn't go to our school.

It was almost a relief to stop this train of thought as I neared the farmhouse and noticed an unfamiliar dark-brown sedan parked in the driveway. Not that this was unusual, since Nona occasionally met with clients at home. With Nona busy, it would be easy to slip unnoticed up to my room.

But as I neared the porch, the front door burst open and Nona stepped out with a man wearing a dark suit. He didn't look like a client. Could this be her potential business partner, Mr. Heart Lights? But he seemed younger than I'd expected, in his thirties instead of closer to my grandmother's age.

"I really can't tell you anything," Nona was saying in a sharp, unfriendly tone. "I'm terribly sorry."

"I doubt that," he said with subtle accusation. Then he saw me and moved quickly, spinning around to stand in front of me, blocking the steps to the house. "And this must be your granddaughter."

Nona gestured toward the dark-brown car, inviting him to leave. "Good luck with your search."

"Are you going to introduce us?" The man stared at me.

Nona smoothed a wrinkle from her yellow skirt, her face calm but her hands had balled into fists. "Mr. Caruthers, this is Sabine."

"Hi," I said politely. His aura, jade greens and browns, gave me a troubled feeling.

"Mr. Caruthers was just leaving," my grandmother added with unusual rudeness.

"I'm in no hurry. I'd like to talk to Sabine." The man's hideous tie hung askew, reminding me of a noose.

"W-Why?" I asked, clasping my hands together.

"Just routine questions," he assured me.

"Mr. Caruthers is a private investigator," Nona added with a warning look.

An investigator? And he wanted to talk to me? Guilt flushed my face. Had the police tracked me down already? Did he know about Jacques and the gun? Something about his tie—a sick shade of orange—bothered me. Hadn't someone recently mentioned an orange tie? As I stared at his tie, my memory clicked.

Was this the PI who was looking for Dominic?

"There's no reason for you to talk to my granddaughter," Nona said sharply.

"It'll only take a few minutes."

"Absolutely not! She's a minor."

"She seems old enough to speak for herself." He tilted his head at me. "Do you mind just a few quick questions?"

Yes, I minded. But refusing would look guilty, like I had something to hide.

"It's okay," I said, giving Nona a look to reassure her

I'd be fine. She shrugged and stepped back, but she continued to frown.

"Do you know Dominic Sarver?" the PI asked me.

"No."

"But you do know a young man named Dominic Smith?"

"Yeah." I tried to sound casual. "I don't know him that well."

"When was the last time you saw him?"

Nona moved beside me, giving me a small jab with her elbow. "I already told Mr. Caruthers that Dominic doesn't work here anymore."

"Right. He doesn't," I echoed. "I haven't seen him for a while."

"Exactly how long?"

"A few days. Maybe a week," I glanced over at Nona who gave me a subtle approving nod.

"Do you know where he went?"

I shook my head. "No."

"Any idea how can I contact him?"

"None at all," I said.

"He's quite an enigma, isn't he? But it's only a matter of time before I track him down." The PI narrowed his gaze at me, then looked over to my grandmother. "Are you sure you can't tell me anything else?"

"If I hear from him, you'll be the first person I call," Nona lied with a sweet smile.

"Yes, I'm sure you will," he said sarcastically. "Tell Mr. Smith—or Sarver—that it would be in his best interests to contact me. He could be the beneficiary of a large estate."

Of course a PI would say that, I thought. Such a pathetic lie! Offer an inheritance to lure out the suspect, then before he can ask "Where's the money?" handcuffs are snapped on and he's listening to a cop read him his rights. I knew better than to believe anything the PI said.

"I'm sure he'll be interested to hear that," Nona said wryly.

"You already have my card, so you know how to reach me." Mr. Caruthers gave a polite bow. "Thank you, ladies, for your time and hospitality."

Nona and I stood silently together, watching him climb into his car and drive away. It wasn't until the car was a small speck in the distance that I turned to my grandmother.

"That was intense." I frowned. "I hope he doesn't come back."

"Don't count on it. I sense we'll be seeing him again, which is unsettling." Nona puckered her lips. "He has a suspicious aura."

"What questions did he ask you?"

"Everything about Dominic—how long I'd known him, when he started working here, and if I'd met any of his relatives."

Lilybelle leapt up to the porch rail and I stroked her soft fur. "So what did you tell him?"

"That Dominic quit his job recently. I insisted that his last name was Smith, not Sarver, and that I'd known his mother so I knew for a fact he didn't have any uncles."

"You didn't really know his mom, did you?" I asked, remembering what Dominic had told me.

"Well, no. I can lie well when I need to," Nona said with a sly wink. "I wanted to make sure the PI stopped looking for him. That story about an inheritance is complete rubbish! If Dominic's parents had money, he wouldn't have been forced to live with that disgusting uncle. That PI can't fool me."

"I didn't believe that story either," I admitted.

"To make sure Mr. Caruthers doesn't show up again, I showed him Dominic's apartment."

"You didn't!"

Nona chuckled. "All he saw was an *empty* loft apartment."

"Empty?" I jerked my hand off Lilybelle, which startled her and caused her to jump off the rail and scamper underneath the chaise lounge. "But what about Dominic's stuff?"

"Hidden." Nona answered gravely. "And so is Dominic."

*   *   *

I had to see for myself.

Jumping off the porch, I raced across the driveway to the barn. I climbed up the stairs and stared into the loft. The walls were missing Dominic's photos and paintings, his favorite books were no longer stacked across shelves, and the dresser top was clean of dust and personal belongings. The only hint that he'd ever lived there was the wooden perch for his falcon, which stood lonely by the open window like the only tree standing in a devastated forest.

When I went back to my grandmother, she refused to tell me where he'd gone. "If he wants you to know, he'll tell you," she said calmly, then walked into her office and shut the door.

If he wants me to know!

I wasn't sure who to be more angry at—my grandmother or Dominic. Didn't they trust me? How dare they shut me out!

Stomping up to my room, I couldn't concentrate on homework or TV or my needlework. To numb my emotions, I jacked up the volume of my stereo.

That's why I didn't know I had a phone call until Nona tapped on my door about an hour later. I didn't call for her to come in because I was still pissed off. But she did anyway. After pausing to turn my music volume way down, she handed me the phone.

I knew it was my father before I heard his voice—and that he was worried about someone in my family.

"Dad?" I tensed. "Is someone sick? Is it Mom?"

"Most people answer with 'hello' or 'how are you doing.'"

"I'm not most people. Are Amy and Ashley okay?"

"Your little sisters are fine, too." Dad cleared his throat. "But I'm not so sure about your older sister."

I tightened my grip on the phone. "Oh?"

"Jade didn't come home last night and her mother is worried."

Biting my lip, I resisted pointing out that Jade's mother was usually the one who caused her daughter to worry. She had a gambling addiction and often left for weeks with no word.

"Crystal called Jade's friends," Dad went on anxiously. "They haven't heard from her and seem to think she was with a new boyfriend, but no one knows."

"Why are you calling me? I barely know Jade."

"I thought you and Jade were getting on better. Amy mentioned you'd been texting each other."

"Well … a little."

"Do you know anything about her new boyfriend?"

Yes, I knew plenty, but did I want to admit this to Dad? Hmmm. I hesitated, thinking, struggling against my bitter emotions, and finally decided I didn't have to tell Dad the awkward stuff. I just told him I'd seen Jade with Evan Marshall yesterday.

"So she's probably still with Evan?

"If not, he'll know where she is." I told him where Evan lived, then we hung up.

Staring at the phone, I resented Jade more than ever. I bet she was creating drama just to stir up trouble. I wasn't worried about her—far from it. She was an inconsiderate bitch who didn't care about anyone else. She wouldn't even take the time to call and let her family know she was with Evan. Or was she with him? Now that I thought back, I'd seen Evan strutting in his usual egotistical way down the hall with some b-ball buddies at school today. If Jade wasn't with him or at her own school, where was she?

I remembered the calls from Jade today that I deleted, and that weird IM she'd sent me: *Wkg on prob. Need 2 talk. Urgent!*

Only I hadn't texted back.

Damn. Now I was feeling guilty. I was furious with Jade but I didn't want anything bad to happen to her. I looked at my phone, but there weren't any new messages and I'd deleted the previous ones efficiently. Maybe she'd emailed.

I checked my computer—and found four emails from her.

The first two just said: *Call me!*

The next one: *Y haven't U called????*

The fourth and last email was dated yesterday at 2:25 p.m.

Sis,
Would U freaking reply?
FYI: Meeting Grey @ 9PM TT 2-nite.
B there.
Jade

Why had Jade met with *Grey*? How had she hooked up with him? And what did "TT" mean? Even more puzzling, why ask me to "B there"?

Only instead of going there, I'd ignored her messages.

She'd gone to meet Grey alone.

And now she was missing.

11

After calling Dad and telling him about the email from Jade, I went to bed early.

Unfortunately, sleep was as elusive as answers to the questions that were buzzing in my mind. It was like someone had pressed the "crazy" button on my life and whirled everything out of control. There must be a curse on names starting with "J." Jade and Josh were missing. And poor Jacques was dead.

When Nona first started training me in how to use my

psychic abilities, she'd talked about the strange mysteries of coincidence. Family members sharing the same birthdays, people dying on the same date they were born, and how you can meet someone and feel like you've known them forever. Most people chalk these happenings up to coincidence, but Nona assured me that there was a master plan for all our lives. Even names, often random, could hold deep meaning to our life paths.

But my worries about Josh and Jade were overshadowed by the hole in my heart left by Dominic. His face was all I saw when I closed my eyes. His voice whispered sweet memories of our special moments together. And my lips ached to feel the soft caress of his again.

To ward off spirits, I always slept with a nightlight on. Tonight I'd chosen a heart-shaped light, and its soft red glow shined across the wall to my bed. Somehow this seemed to calm my anxiety, as if the heart's light connected me to Dominic.

The next morning, I was surprised at how soundly I'd slept. No dreams of guns, dead bodies, or evil magicians who could make people disappear. Although I immediately remembered everything as soon as I opened my eyes. Getting ready for school seemed like such a futile, ordinary thing. But what else could I do?

Besides, I had a test in English.

I was a little disappointed when Penny-Love didn't show up to pick me up, so I texted her. She responded: "CU@L8R."

When I got to school, I found her waiting for me—only she wasn't alone.

Thorn's pink fishnet stockings, chalky makeup, and tiny metal skull earrings were a stark contrast to Penny-Love's skinny jeans with flower-shaped pockets, empire waist striped blouse, and hair snagged in two bouncy red ponytails.

"You two together?" I asked.

"A lapse of sanity," Thorn answered, scowling.

"We need to stick together—at least until this little problem is over," Penny-Love said.

"Little?" Thorn mocked.

"Give me a break, okay? I've had a bad night." Penny-Love's eyes were puffy and shadowed as if she'd slept badly. "Sabine, have you heard anything?"

"About what?"

Looking around furtively, Penny-Love hissed in my ear, "Jacques! What else?"

"Oh ... yeah. And no, I haven't heard anything."

"Me neither! And it's making me insane!" She grasped my arm, her nails sharp against my skin. "I checked the news and there was nothing about Jacques at all! How can that be? No reports about the murder of a local high school student?"

"I told you we should have called 911," I retorted. "His body probably hasn't been discovered."

"Oh yes it has," Penny-Love assured me.

"How can you be so sure? It's not like you went back to check..." I watched a guilty blush darken her face. "Ohmygod, Pen—you didn't!"

"I had to. After Thorn went home, I couldn't stop thinking about Jacques. I just had to know. So I drove back, expecting to see police cars and flashing lights. But it was calm. So I went into the apartment building...just to check."

"You idiot!" Thorn glared. "You deserve to be on that TV show about stupid criminals."

"But I'm not a criminal." Penny-Love's shoulders shook like she was close to breaking down.

"We know that," I assured her as I slipped my arm around her. I shot a venomous look at Thorn. "Right, Thorn?"

"Oh, all right," Thorn said ungraciously. "She's not a criminal. She's just acting stupid."

"I couldn't help myself," Penny-Love sobbed. "I had to know what was going on and to make sure someone found him. I was careful and pretended like I was going to a different apartment. His apartment door was closed and I heard voices inside. So I figured it was the police, although I wondered why there wasn't any of that murder-site tape you always see on TV shows when they find a dead body."

"TV shows aren't always accurate about stuff like that," Thorn put in.

"Still, it couldn't have been the police, because I checked online and there is not one single mention of Jacques' murder. I couldn't find anything at all on him. It's like he wasn't just killed—he was erased from existence."

"Weirdness." Thorn furrowed her brow.

"I can't forget him, and I have to know what happened."

"It'll eventually make the news," I assured Penny-Love.

"What if it doesn't?" she argued, with a fierceness that surprised me. "What if his killer goes free?"

"Stuff happens." Thorn shrugged.

"Not to people I care about," Penny-Love insisted. "I can't wait around without doing anything. I keep remembering Jacques—how he laughed, or the cute way he scrunched his face in concentration when he painted, and how his arms felt so warm and his hands knew exactly—"

"Stop right there!" Purple fingernails flashed as Thorn's hand flew up in protest. "I don't want to hear about your sex life."

"Not sex … romance." A sad smile flickered across Penny-Love's face. "And he was the best … even if all he could talk about was partying and getting high. He was a little dangerous, but a real good guy. That's why I asked you both here—because I'm going to find out who killed him and I need you both to help."

I shook my head. "I just can't … there's too much

going on for me. Josh is missing and maybe Jade, too. And Thorn saw that folder with Josh's picture in Jacques' apartment—what's up with that? Then there's Dominic... well, he needs me too. My worry quota is so maxed out I can't handle more problems. Leave the murder to the cops."

"But you're my best friend, Sabine," Penny-Love whined. "You can't desert me now that I'm in my most desperate situation ever."

When she put it like that, it was hard to refuse. I wavered.

"Lose the martyr act," Thorn snapped at Penny-Love.

"What's that supposed to mean?" Penny-Love retorted.

"If you're any kind of friend to Sabine, you'd notice that she's going through some rough stuff, too. But all you can think about is yourself, as usual."

"I didn't ask for your opinion."

"But you were about to ask for my help, which means Finding. That's something you promised never to mention again."

"I didn't mention it," Penny-Love said, glaring. "You did."

"You were going to."

"So what if I was? But obviously you won't help me."

"Once again you're wrong, Cheerleader." Thorn was shorter than Penny-Love, but somehow she seemed taller with her gold, green, and amber-red aura shimmering bright. "I'll help you, not that you deserve it, but because I don't want you hassling Sabine."

"I wasn't—"

"Don't deny it. You were playing on her soft heart, expecting her to follow you like a minion. She didn't find the body, we did. If you're serious about wanting to find Jacque's killer, we leave her out of this. I can help more than Sabine. Are you in or not?"

"Well ..." Penny-Love glanced at me, frowning. Then she blew out a deep breath and turned back to Thorn. "I'm in."

*   *   *

Thorn's support surprised me and got me thinking about friendships as I walked slowly to my next class. Was Penny-Love really my best friend? Sometimes she acted like it, but mostly she was focused on her own drama. She was fun and popular, and her gift of gab was good camouflage for my freaky gifts. Hanging out with her made it easy to slip into the background of the semi-popular crowd without being noticed. Was that the description of a best friend?

The funny thing, I realized later, as I caught a glimpse of Thorn with one of her Goth friends, was that Thorn was acting more like my best friend. She'd come to my defense and criticized Pen for bossing me around. It was easy to be with her, too, because she accepted me without judgment. Yet Thorn never introduced me to her Goth friends and we didn't hang out like real friends. Sometimes the only way I knew what she was doing was when I'd asked Manny—which is what I did when I saw him during lunch in the computer room.

"Does Thorn have a best friend?"

"Thorn doesn't have a best anything." The beads in Manny's dreads rattled as he turned away from the computer. "Why do you ask?"

"I was just thinking..."

"Dangerous thing to do," he teased. "Could land you in all kinds of trouble."

"I'm in plenty already."

"Anything you want to talk about?"

I sighed. It was tempting to confide in him since he'd helped me out many times. But telling the editor of the school newspaper that a classmate was murdered and I knew where the murder weapon was hidden would not be a smart move. Of course, not reporting the murder wasn't smart either. But everything had happened so fast and we'd panicked.

"Come on, Beany," he said, using his ridiculous nickname for me. "Is this about Josh? Is he still missing?"

"How did you know about that?"

He smiled mysteriously. "Mystic Manny sees and knows all."

"I see and know all about Manny being a big fake."

"There is a supreme talent to the art of faking, which I excel at," he bragged. "My prediction column is hugely popular."

"Did you forget who supplies you with all the predictions?"

"I can never forget you, Beany."

"Don't call me that."

"Are you stressing over Josh?" Manny patted my hand sympathetically. "Because he's gone and no one knows where he is?"

"I am worried," I admitted, deciding it was safe to tell him about that problem. So I filled him in on the trip to Josh's house: Horse not eating, the note Josh left behind, the weird vision I'd gotten by touching the wand, and Thorn's vague Finding results for Josh.

"Hmmm," he said when I finished, stroking the faint dark stubble on his chin. "Well, my wise girl, you have come to the right place. I'm positive I can find Josh."

"How?"

"Intensive analysis and research," he said, gesturing toward a computer. "Focus on the facts. Josh was being secretive about his magician activities. He had recently broken up with his girlfriend—you."

My cheeks reddened. "Our breakup had nothing to do with his disappearance."

"I didn't say it did; just compiling the facts. What was his reaction to your split?"

"He avoided me and wouldn't return my messages."

"A traumatic break-up can result in extreme behavior—like running away."

"He didn't run away!" I snapped. "I'm afraid Grey did something to him. I told you about Grey—how he vandalized Trick and Treats but then conned Josh into thinking he was innocent."

"How do you know Josh is with Grey?"

"His note said he left with Arturo, but a witness saw him get into a car with Grey."

"What witness?"

I hesitated, because I knew this would sound out there even for me. "Josh's dog. Dominic talked to him and dogs never lie."

"A dog is *not* a reliable witness," Manny said with a swish of his dreads, spinning in his chair, fingers flying across the keyboard. "Still, Josh is probably with *both* Arturo and Grey. All the evidence hints at some kind of magician hideaway in the woods. Thorn's map clue is useful, too. I'll look into this for you and you'll—"

"And I'll come up with the twelve new Ten Years in the Future predictions," I said, sighing.

"Have you started on them yet?" he persisted.

"No. But I predict that in ten years I may have it done."

"Not funny." Manny stood up, slipping an arm around my shoulder. "You meditate or whatever you need to do, and I'll get on the Josh problem. He's a cool dude and I always liked him. I want to find him, too."

But what about Jacques? I wondered. Did he have any friends or family looking for him? No one at school seemed to notice he was gone. Dead. What would have happened if I'd meditated on his future a few days ago? Would I have seen what would happen to him? Could I have saved him?

"Deliver the predictions by Thursday at noon," Manny was saying.

I hesitated then nodded. "I'll do my best."

"Great! This is going to be an amazing column. I won't even tell you who to write about. Pick anyone, even teachers if you want."

He handed me last year's Sheridan High yearbook.

*   *   *

I walked home from school, since Penny-Love had texted me that she was going off with Thorn. I didn't ask where; I didn't want to know.

All I wanted was Dominic back in his loft apartment, waiting for me.

But his truck was still missing and there was a sense of emptiness around the barn. In my heart, I knew he was really gone.

A part of me was gone, too.

He hadn't even said good-bye. Not even a crummy text message. Hearts do break and die, I thought miserably. Even though I had a long list of things to do when I got home, I felt aimless and empty. I longed to hide in my room, shut the door and turn off the light, and disappear into sleep.

I started up the front porch, then stopped.

What was that mewing sound?

Looking around, I saw Lilybelle jump down from the porch rail and hurry toward me. Her multi-colored tail was swishing back and forth.

She looked up and mewed loudly; this was not her usual request to be petted, but a demanding sound. I set my backpack on the porch swing and reached down to pick her up. She squirmed a few feet away. Then she stopped to stare back at me.

"What's with you?" I murmured.

She meowed with attitude, then moved farther away and once again stopped, giving me a demanding, pleading expression.

"Are you hungry?"

She twitched her tail.

"I take that as a no," I said, puzzled.

She kept circling in an agitated manner. I wished Dominic were here to decipher her language. I'd never had any luck trying to understand animals.

"So what do you want?"

Lilybelle pounced over to my feet and started chewing on my shoelaces.

"Hey, stop that! These are my best sneakers!"

I reached down and pushed her away from my shoes.

She nipped at my fingers, not actually biting. Then she scampered away a few feet and paused with a demanding twitch of her whiskers.

"Do you want me to follow you?"

She waved her tail up and down like a nod.

So I followed.

She led me past the barn, through the corral and across the pasture where horses and cows grazed. She didn't slow down, either, hurrying on her four little legs as if she was in a race. I had to run to keep up with her. When we came to the edge of my grandmother's property, the fence that bordered the woods, Lilybelle jumped over the gate.

"I hope you know where you're going," I grumbled as I heaved myself up on the gate and jumped down on the other side.

She was disappearing down a narrow path that led into the woods, and I followed at full speed. I lost her a few times, but then saw her colorful tail. The trees all around us came together in a shady, dark canopy, and the dirt trail made by wild animals was extremely hard to follow.

Then suddenly, Lilybelle stopped in front of a tree trunk that was as large as a refrigerator, dark and gnarled with rough bark. I stopped, too, bending over to catch my breath and beginning to feel like a total idiot for following my cat into the woods. It would be dark soon, and I didn't dare stay long or I might not find my way back out until morning. While we weren't high enough in elevation to have bears, there were mountain lions here—distant DNA relatives of Lilybelle who I did *not* want to meet.

Where was Lilybelle, anyway?

I glanced around, not seeing any sign of my calico.

There was a rustling sound and something soft landed on my shoulder. Reaching up, I picked off a leaf. Then I tilted back my head and looked up, up, up into the tree, expecting to see my cat.

Instead, I saw sandy-brown hair and blue eyes.

"About time you showed up," Dominic said.

Then he reached down and lifted me into the tree.

12

I stared in astonishment as my feet landed, not on a branch, but on carpet.

"Welcome to my humble abode," Dominic said, not letting go of my hand. I didn't let go either, enjoying his warm, firm, wonderful touch.

"A tree house?" I asked. Not a crude tree house made of sticks and boards, but an airborn cabin with sturdy walls, a kitchen nook, a patched leather couch, and a rocking chair underneath the gray-blue halo of a skylight. A light brightened inside of me, too, knowing that Dominic had brought me here, that he wanted to see me.

"Like it?" Dominic grinned.

"It's amazing! Did you build it?"

"No."

"So who did?"

"Your grandmother."

"Nona? No way!"

"Don't underestimate her," Dominic said, leading me to the couch and gesturing for me to sit down. He sat close beside me. "She told me it was her retreat when being a mother and wife stressed her out and she needed a private place of her own."

"That was like decades ago!" I looked around, still overwhelmed by this miniature home in a tree. "It's been here since before I was even born? But I used to play in these woods and I never noticed a tree house."

"It's camouflaged well," Dominic said.

"Like a magician's illusion." I stared around in astonishment.

"No lame stage tricks here, just clever construction. Branches have grown around the walls, and this tree is an evergreen variety that doesn't lose its leaves. When you look up from the ground, all you see is a jumble of thick, gnarled branches."

"Wow. How did Nona get that up here?" I pointed to a mini-fridge.

"She didn't—I brought it when I knew I might be staying here for a while. It runs on propane."

"Does Nona bring you food?"

"No. She's paranoid about the PI and thinks he might be spying on us with high-tech equipment. She doesn't even want me using a cell phone. So my animal posse helps out." He gave a shrill whistle and dark wings fluttered through an open window. His falcon landed on a wooden post.

"What does Dagger do?" I asked.

"Relays messages."

"Apparently so does Lilybelle." At the sound of her name, my cat lifted her tail proudly and rubbed against my legs, purring.

"Lily's cool," Dominic said, smiling. "I would have sent Dagger but he was out hunting."

"Hunting food for you?" I asked, a little grossed out by that mental image.

"Nah, I'm not that desperate yet." Dominic chuckled. He walked over to the fridge and opened it to show left-over cartons from fast food restaurants. "When I want to go out, Dagger unlatches the corral so Rio can gallop here. Then I ride him to my truck—it's hidden at the edge of the woods near the road."

"You ride a horse to your truck?"

"A horse pulling up to a drive-through window would draw attention," he joked. "Last night I got Chinese."

Then he invited me to share sweet and sour pork, noodles, and veggie leftovers.

We ate, played cards, and talked. I was surprised to find out he'd even gone back to Josh's house.

"How's Horse?" I asked.

"Much better—and not because of anything I did."

"So who helped him?

Dominic set down the hand of cards he was holding and gave me a look that warned me I wouldn't like what he was about to say. "Evan. He's been taking care of Horse— feeding and walks at the park."

"Well … that's good," I said begrudgingly. It was hard not to hate Evan, even when he did something nice. "What about Josh? Any news?"

"Yeah." Dominic nodded. "Good news—he called his parents."

"Oh my god, huge relief! What did he say?"

"That he'd be back by Christmas."

"Mrs. DeMarco must be thrilled."

"Yeah. She was. What about you?" It was a question, and not a light one.

"I'm glad he's okay … but only because he's still a friend." I met his look. "Nothing more."

"Good," he said, picking up his cards, checking them, then discarding one in the center pile on the table.

"Did Josh explain anything?" I picked up his discarded card and added it to my hand. "Like why he'd left and where he was?"

"Only that he was with Arturo for secret magician training."

"Why all the secrecy?"

"You don't want to hear my opinion," Dominic said.

"Anyway, it's great that Horse is better—one less thing for you to deal with."

"Yeah. He'll be all right."

But will you? I thought, thinking of the PI.

Except for the rustling leaves outside the tree house and unseen creatures whispering across branches, the air inside our haven grew silent. I stiffened, inches away from my love yet feeling as if I was slipping away from him.

"So with Horse okay, you can leave," I said, fighting not to cry. "You've kept your promise to help and now there's no reason for you to stay."

"There's you." He tugged on my hand and drew me into his arms, whispering a kiss. "I don't want to leave."

"You'll stay?"

"As long as I can."

Then he pulled me closer, our hearts beating in sync, and there was no more talk about Josh, Horse, or leaving.

During school the next day, I replayed my wonderful evening with Dominic. Thinking about him made me feel less alone, like he walked along with me.

With only a few more days of school until Christmas vacation, not much happened in my classes and even less on break and lunch. Thorn and Penny-Love were mysteriously absent. When I texted Pen to ask what was going on, her replies were very cryptic. I knew it had something to do with Jacques. There still hadn't been any news about his murder, and no one at school seemed to be aware he was gone. Normally I'd ask Manny to use his hacker skills to check online, only I couldn't tell him about the murder… if it *was* murder. I was starting to doubt my vision of Jacques' bloody body. It wouldn't be the first time I'd misinterpreted a vision—there was the time I'd astral-traveled to Jade's house and thought something horrible had happened to her mother. But Crystal turned out to be fine.

I didn't dwell on this for long because the clock was ticking down the minutes to my rendezvous with Dominic that evening and my thoughts were all about love. I just wanted to be with Dominic in every way. Images would flash in my mind—and not the psychic variety. I'd be sitting in class, watching my teacher write on the board, when suddenly I'd imagine Dominic's face or shirtless body. I'd feel his touch on my skin, his lips on my mouth, and the heat of our bodies close together.

And I wondered what it might be like to *really* be with Dominic. I'd never gotten that close to any guy before and to be honest, I wasn't sure if I was ready. Still, I kept thinking how getting that serious would bond Dominic to me so securely he'd never leave. Our hiding place in the woods was completely private (except for feathered and furry visitors). High above the ground, sounds muffled by leaves and branches, we could do whatever we wanted...oh...and how I *wanted.*

Dominic hadn't made any moves, though, which confused me. Didn't he feel the same way? My longings were hot enough to spontaneously combust the tree house, but Dominic never asked for more than hand-holding and kissing. Even with my psychic connection to Dominic, I didn't know what he was thinking.

After school I couldn't wait to get home. But I had to wait till dark to sneak out so that no one would see me. When it was finally late enough, I took extra time brushing my hair into loose waves rather than twisting it into a braid, and I wore a sexy tank top under a silky low-V sweater and low-rider jeans. I knew Dominic wasn't big into makeup so I only dabbed on peach gloss.

With only glowing cat eyes to guide me, I found my way to the tree house. I loved the way he looked at me. His gaze darkened, deep with something I hoped was desire. But then he just sat down at the table and started shuffling cards.

Not the game I had in mind.

But I could wait...

Dominic taught me thirty-one different versions of poker and I came close to suggesting #32: strip poker. Bad, bad, Sabine, I thought to myself. Instead, I taught him a game I'd learned from Nona called "Spit and Cuss." We didn't spit, but I cussed a little when he won four times in a row.

And we laughed a lot, especially at the silly antics of Dominic's animal posse. Hanging out in a tree seemed to give the wild life an open invitation. A chubby squirrel and a scrawny squirrel bickered over a nut as they chased each other across the branchy ceiling. Dominic tried to solve this by offering them a second nut, but the scrawny squirrel grabbed both nuts then scurried out the window. Other animals stopped by, too—an owl with a white heart-shaped face, a raccoon with an adorable baby, and even a skunk (Dominic assured me she was tame and wouldn't stink-bomb me, but I still refused to pet her.).

Lots of wildlife, but nothing wild happening with me and Dominic. Seriously frustrating.

When I got back home, I channeled my pent-up energy into coming up with twelve predictions for Manny. Meditation was relaxing and opened my psyche, so that when I flipped through the yearbook Manny had given me, it was easier than I'd expected to glimpse the future. I finished twelve predictions, and during lunch break the next day in the computer room, I proudly handed them to Manny. When he read through the names I'd chosen—mostly mutual friends, a teacher, and even one for Manny—he threw back his head and laughed. This article was definitely going to stir things up around school, he told me. He couldn't wait for Friday.

I couldn't wait till Friday, either, but for completely different reasons. Dominic didn't know it yet, but I'd decided that evening would mark the beginning of a deeper love between us.

Friday dragged on like each second was a decade. We had substitutes in two of my classes, which meant more messing around than learning. Jill, head cheerleader, invited me to join the squad for lunch, which was cool but awkward when she asked about Penny-Love, who was still mysteriously absent.

I shook my head. "No idea what's up with that girl."

Fortunately, there was plenty of other news buzzing during lunch. The *Sheridan Shout-Out* special issue had been printed and there was lots of drama over Mystic Manny's future predictions. I smiled whenever I heard someone gasp, "Is Mr. Blankenship really going to get rich?" Or, "No way is Kaitlyn going into the Army!"

But beyond my smile, something deep was simmering.

And that evening, when Dominic lifted me into the tree house, the touch of his fingers shocked electricity through me. The heat between us was so intense that Dominic would have to have been a robot not to notice.

But his only reaction was a glance at the food sack I was carrying. "What did you bring?" he asked.

I brought *me*, I wanted to shout.

"Fried chicken," I told him.

"Hmmm, smells great. You hungry too?"

"Oh yes." But not for food.

He put paper plates on the lopsided coffee table and offered me a cold drink from his fridge. I scooted very close beside him on the ripped couch.

"Nona sent you a message," I told him, wiping my greasy fingers on my jeans.

"What?"

"About the PI," I said seriously. "Nona talked to a clerk at the Valley View Hotel and found out that Mr. Caruthers is checking out tomorrow. Isn't that great news?"

Dominic chewed and shook his head.

"But aren't you relieved? With the PI gone, everything can go back to normal."

"I don't think so," he told me.

"Why not?"

"I'm still a wanted man."

"Wanted, yes." I nodded, scooting close to him on the couch. "By me."

"I want to be with you, too." He reached up to touch my cheek, softly. "But you deserve better."

"No one is better for me than you."

"How can you say that, knowing what I did?"

"Because I know who you are. Here." I touched my hand to my heart.

He followed my gesture, so close that I could feel the heat flaring between us. But he drew back with a shake of his head. "I wish things were different."

"I don't," I told him. "You're who you are because of your past, and we'll get through your problems together."

"Sabine ..." My name fell like a caress from his lips.

"You need to let me go."

"All I need is you."

"I won't drag you into my mess."

"You didn't drag me—I'm here willingly. Don't you get it? I want to be with you no matter how much trouble you're in." I leaned against him, our thighs touching. "I welcome *your* trouble."

"Sabine, why do you make me so crazy?"

"Do I?" I asked innocently, resting my head on his shoulder.

"So very, very ..." He sucked in a ragged breath, staring deep into my face. "Very crazy."

My skin trembled when his finger traced my jaw, lingering near my lips. My whole world was focused on his hands, his wonderful, rough, tanned hands. I sank against his warmth as his strong arms folded around me, drawing me only a breath away, a sweet cinnamon breath as if he'd eaten a pastry recently. I had the urge to taste his lips and—

Thump!

Sharp claws dug into my lap.

"Lilybelle!" I cried, jumping up. "Bad kitty!"

"Can't blame her for wanting your attention," Dominic said, scratching my cat under her scruff.

"It's not my attention she wants. It's yours. She's jealous."

"How do you know?" he chuckled. "Can you speak her language?"

"No, but I'd love to learn. Can you teach me how to talk to her, too, so she'll obey me?"

"No one can make a cat obey. The trick is to convince them they want to do what you want them to do. Communication with animals isn't about knowing the right words, it's much more subtle."

"I'm all for subtle communicating." I nudged Lilybelle off his lap. Grasping Dominic's hand, I brought his rough skin to my lips for a not-so-subtle kiss.

He slipped his arm around my shoulders, drawing me closer. I lifted my chin and his lips caressed my own, soft and sweet yet with a taste of wild, too. And my emotions boiled, tumbled, and intensified.

"If I asked for something," I whispered, "would you refuse?"

"I can never refuse you."

"So, do you want to ... well ..." My face burned. "You know."

"Huh?" He scrunched his brow. "What?"

"I mean ... don't you want anything from me?"

He gestured to the fried chicken. "You already brought me food."

Were guys really this clueless?

I was half on his lap, leaning in so my lips were a whisper from his. "Dominic, don't you know what I'm trying to say? Only Nona knows we're here and she won't interrupt us."

"You know why?" He looked deeply into my face, searching. When I only shook my head, he went on. "Nona trusts us. I don't want to lose her respect."

"Nona doesn't have to know... if there's anything to know," I added, blushing. "We're alone in our private paradise. Anything can happen."

He touched my cheek with one finger, tracing my jaw down to my lips. "Are you sure you want *anything* to happen?"

I caught the husky fiber of his tone and fell deep into the blue waters of his eyes. I understood that I was at an intersection, one of those life paths that Opal often hinted at, where the choices that were made could change everything. I mentally paused, listening for my spirit guide's voice, expecting her to butt in with her usual preachy advice. But I only heard the drum beat of my own heart. She'd abandoned me to adult choices.

And I wasn't a child anymore; I was almost an adult, and ready to be completely a woman. I trusted Dominic even more than myself. All that existed for me in this moment was Dominic. Here, with me, his heart open and his hands on my skin. Softly moving, fingers reaching, his mouth whispering in my ear.

"Being with you feels so right," I murmured. "But I want so much more."

"More, what?" His lips brushed against my forehead, my nose, my lips.

"More *you*. Only you."

"You have me."

"Do I?" My voice caught as I saw beyond his words, to an image of him driving his truck on a lonely road far away. "I have this feeling that you're still planning to leave."

"I don't want to."

"Stay here and we'll hide together," I told him. "The animals can bring anything we need, and we could be happy here forever."

"Until another investigator or the police show up."

"What would it take to make you stay? I'll do anything."

He cupped my face in his strong, rough hands, staring deep and hard into my soul. My own emotions were so insane with desire, fear, and joy that I couldn't see beyond them into his mind. What was he thinking? Did he know how far I'd go to keep him with me? I'd give myself completely to him, not only because I loved him so much but because I was sure that it would keep him here longer. Anything, anything... he only had to nod.

Instead, he shook his head and turned away.

There was a silence in the tree house that lingered like long barren seasons ... spring blossoms dying, summer's burning heart, fall's loss of innocence, and brutal winter reality.

"Dominic?" I said tentatively.

He didn't answer. His aura was charcoal gray and smol-dering-fire crimson.

"Please," I whispered, shifting on the couch toward him. His face, twisted in anguish, broke my heart. "Tell me what you're thinking."

His granite gaze was distant, as if he'd gone far away while his body was still here. Fear slithered up my spine. When he reached for my hand, his skin sweaty hot, I knew something had changed.

"It all comes down to respect," he finally said. "I don't deserve any from you or Nona if I don't respect myself, too. And I can't respect someone who dumps his problems on the people he cares about and hides from his own mis-takes."

"You're not like that. You didn't do anything wrong."

"I killed my uncle whether I meant to or not," he said, in a chilly winter tone.

"What are you going to do?" I asked, my fears rising.

"Face my demons." His gaze swept around the room as if he was seeing it for the last time. "Tomorrow I'll go to the PI and turn myself in."

13

I begged Dominic to let me call my father so he could
have a lawyer protect his rights, but he refused. "I'll handle this on my own," he insisted.

"Then let me go with you," I argued.

But he refused that, too. "I don't want you or your
family involved," he said stubbornly.

"But loving you makes me involved! Nona too."

"That's exactly why I don't want to burden you with

this. I've been running for five years, since I was a boy. But I'm a man now, and I need to face this on my own."

"You're shutting me out. That's not fair."

"Don't make this harder than it already is."

"I just want to help you," I said, my voice cracking.

"You can't." There was a bleakness in his gaze that hurt my heart. "Please, go."

I stared at him. "Is that what you really want?"

When he nodded, it was like a door had been slammed in my face. There was no talking Dominic out of his decision.

Fine! If that's what he wanted, I'd leave. And I did.

Without even a good-bye.

Alone in my bedroom, I totally regretted leaving and nearly ran back through the woods to Dominic. But what if he turned me away again?

Tonight was supposed to have been all about becoming closer to Dominic. Yet now we were farther apart than ever. Life would be all sorts of awful when Dominic turned himself in to the PI. I would try again to convince him to let my father help, but it all seemed so hopeless. Dominic had admitted to killing his uncle. His whole future—our future together—was over before it even started. Arrested, locked up for months, years ... life? I saw myself growing old and alone, fading from blond to gray and never knowing love again.

To comfort myself as I got ready for bed, I chose an eagle-shaped nightlight, which was the closest I had to a falcon. Dominic was meant to be free like a wild creature, not caged without sky and sunshine. I had to stop him from ruining his life. I tossed and turned, tempted so many times to fly out of bed and return to the tree house.

At the edges of my mind, a dark-haired woman called my name. But I pushed Opal out, not wanting to hear her say things like *Being honest is its own reward* and *This will be for the best.*

"Go away," I thought to her. And she did.

Somehow I managed to sleep through the night, waking later than usual. It was Saturday, the first day of winter vacation. Through my window, I could see the morning shimmering in frost diamonds across the tree tops. I got up and dressed warmly, putting on my heaviest shoes and two pairs of socks, then grabbed a down-lined jacket. I felt the urge to hurry, hurry! There was no time to waste getting to Dominic.

I hadn't found any solutions in my tormented dreams, except an understanding that hurt feelings didn't matter when you loved someone.

So I went to find Dominic.

But when I got there, the tree house was empty. No birds, squirrels, or rustles from other wild creatures. All I found was a note pinned to the tree trunk.

My Sabine,
Sorry for what I said.
Please respect what I have to do.
I'll always love you,
Your Dominic

I read this over and over. In my mind I could hear him say "My Sabine" like a whispered kiss. He loved me. I loved him. Why couldn't that be enough?

When I tried his cell, it went straight to voicemail.

What had Nona said about the PI? That he was checking out of his hotel today? Dominic couldn't have left too long ago; his aura and the faint scent of coffee lingered in the tree house. So if I hurried back, I could go to that hotel and stop him.

"Nona!" I called, as I bursting into the house.

I found my grandmother in her room, sitting in bed with a sleepy look. "What is it?" she asked, reaching over for her glasses. "Are you okay?"

"It's not me—it's Dominic. He's turning himself in to the PI!"

Nona was out of bed quickly, slipping a robe over her purple silk pajamas. She led me to the kitchen and turned on the hot water. Instead of rushing off after Dominic, she made tea and invited me to sit at the table. When I protested, she placed a comforting hand on my shoulder and assured me that we wouldn't sit by and do nothing. We'd make sure Dominic had a good lawyer, no matter what he wanted. Then she held me. And we cried together.

I couldn't eat anything, so I just went to my room. I curled up on the window seat with a blanket around my shoulders and stared out at the barn.

My thoughts were numb, as if the chilly weather outside had invaded my heart. This should be a happy, festive time. Two whole weeks of vacation, holiday gatherings with family and friends ... but no Dominic.

I kept glancing at my cell phone, willing him to call me. But there weren't any calls—not even from Jade.

Jade ... what was going on with her, anyway?

With Dominic leaving, it had slipped my mind that Jade was in some kind of trouble, too. Of course, by now she was probably home. Curious, I called my father.

Still missing, Dad told me. His voice was sharp with anxiety. He'd contacted Evan, but that was a dead end (I cringed at those words). Evan said he hadn't seen or heard from Jade. I asked Dad if the email from Jade had been any help, but he said he'd had no luck tracking down Grey. He wasn't going to give up, though, and would let me know if anything new came up.

After I hung up the phone, I opened my email and reread Jade's last note. I stared hard at the words: ... *FYI: Meeting Grey @ 9PM TT 2-nite.*

That was Sunday night, almost a week ago. But what was "TT"? Since Jade was the paranoid type, they must have met someplace where Jade would feel safe, and also that Grey could easily find. A place both of them had been before...

I snapped my fingers. Of course!

I knew exactly where they'd met.

And I was going there, too.

*   *   *

Nona was leaning back in her office chair, talking on the phone. I waited for her to notice me, then asked to borrow her car. She nodded and tossed me the keys. She waved but didn't ask any questions, just returned to her call.

I had my hand on the door ready to leave when I felt a poke in my side. Looking around, I didn't see anyone, but I sensed a presence and heard a whisper calling me.

"Opal, I don't have time for you now," I told my spirit guide, shutting my eyes so I could clearly see her golden skin, critically arched black brows, and braided hair coiled into a crown.

If I can cross unimaginable boundaries to reach you, it would serve you well to make a moment for conversation, Opal lectured me.

"I'm in a hurry," I insisted.

Haste creates missed opportunities. Adhere to my advice or suffer the agony of regret.

I sighed. Sarcasm was a highly evolved art for Opal. "What do you want now?"

To protect you from an unscrupulous enemy and cushion your crossings at a dangerous intersection. By giving yourself away to save another, you may lose your Earth life and find yourself lost among the living dead.

"What are the living dead?"

It is my fervent hope you never find out. Under no circumstances should you leave your dwelling, and you will then escape the gray winds of the gathering storm.

"I can't sit around here doing nothing," I argued.

The cusp of darkest night draws near and if you stray from your safe haven, you will face dire consequences.

"What consequences?" I asked, annoyed.

The window of warning is dim, without much information. Words come to me, and I'll share them although I do not fathom their meaning: "Hold close the crystal staff to save heart, or the old soul seeking to command death will steal beyond life."

"Huh? I totally don't get it."

Perhaps not now, but dwell on it at a future moment for protection.

"Do you enjoy confusing me?"

I do not enjoy your lack of appreciation and comprehension, which is to be expected in one limited by the gravity of ignorance.

I had a feeling she was calling me stupid, but it was hard to tell.

What old soul? What crystal staff? Could Opal possibly mean the cheap magic wand I'd found in Josh's room?

I started to laugh because the idea was so ridiculous. The wand wasn't crystal, it was plastic.

Before I could ask Opal, I sensed her drawing away; having confused me completely, she was leaving. So typical! I stood with my hand still on the doorknob for a moment, trying to decide whether or not to bring the silly magic wand, then finally decided that it wouldn't hurt to have it with me. So I ran upstairs, tossed it in my tote bag, and headed for the neighborhood candy shop.

TT = Trick or Treats.

*   *   *

Do criminals have a demented desire to return to the scene of their crime? I wondered about this as I made the short drive to Trick or Treats. And I could now understand why Penny-Love felt compelled to go back to Jacques' apartment.

But why would Grey meet Jade at the shop he'd vandalized? Coming back was risky—he could be recognized. Then again, the cocky jerk probably thought he was too smart to be caught. My brief glimpse into his aura had shown me splashes of the brazen red and charcoal black of reckless behavior and a damaged soul.

The brick building that housed Trick or Treats was half-hidden at the end of Maple Street. On the surface, Velvet's store was just a candy shop filled with cases of mouthwatering chocolates and other delicious goodies, but if she invited you into the back room, you'd find a different kind of shop—one with crystals, candles, herbs, and a large collection of New Age and paranormal books.

Since it was still early, Trick or Treats wasn't open yet. But Velvet's car was there, so I knew she had to be inside. I knocked loudly and called out for her.

"Why, Sabine, what a lovely surprise," Velvet said in her British lilt, her high heels clicking on the tile in a cheerful rhythm. She wore snug designer slacks with elegant jewelry and her hair was swept up in a chignon.

"Sorry to bother you so early," I said, with a wistful glance at a glass case of caramel marshmallows decorated like wrapped holiday gifts.

"It's no bother at all. I'm delighted to see you." Velvet's smile lit up her usually prim-and-proper face as she ushered me inside. Her skin was smooth and ageless, making it impossible to tell if she was in her thirties or fifties.

"I need to ask you something," I told her, unsure how to begin. Sweet scents of chocolate, vanilla, and caramel made my stomach grumble.

"Ask away. I do hope your dear grandmother isn't feeling unwell."

"Oh, Nona's doing great. Her health has never been better and her business is booming, too. She's met a man who's interested in merging his own dating service with Soul-Mate Matches."

"Good for her." Velvet gestured for me to sit beside her at a round marble table. "Now tell me about your problem. Your energy is heavy and troubled."

"My half-sister Jade is missing," I began, then launched into the whole story about Jade meeting Grey here.

"That boy was the vandal?" she exclaimed, clutching the edge of the table with a shaking hand. "I thought he seemed familiar, but I couldn't place him. I did recognize Jade, though, since she looks so much like you."

"So they *did* come here?"

"Oh, yes. Jade sat at that table over there, sipping a vanilla raspberry soda and staring out the window. I asked if she was waiting for someone and she told me she was meeting a friend. We sat for a few moments and chatted. I offered her a complimentary toffee sunburst bar. She was very gracious and thanked me."

"Then what happened?"

Velvet frowned. "She waited for over an hour. I had a gathering scheduled so I had to close the shop up early. I didn't want to rush her, though, and worried that she was being stood up. Just as I was about to go over and talk to her, the pale, tall boy came in."

"Grey," I whispered.

"His energy disturbed me," Velvet said with a shiver. "I was surprised your sister didn't introduce us."

"Jade and I may share DNA, but not much else," I said, scowling. "What happened next?"

"They left and I had the meeting."

"In the back room?" I guessed, remembering when I'd gone there for a séance.

"Yes." Velvet nodded. "Friends from my coven. So I don't know any more about Jade. But I'm worried about her going off with that disturbing young man."

"I'm worried, too," I said, nodding. "Jade hasn't been seen or heard from since Sunday evening."

"That's when they were here." Velvet bit her lip. "Have the police been called?"

"I don't think so—not yet, anyway. With Jade, you can't be sure what's going on." I hesitated, not sure how much to reveal about my dysfunctional family. "Her mother takes off for weeks at a time with no contact. Jade may be doing something like that."

"That girl has jumped head first into trouble. I can feel it."

I could feel it too.

"Well, I better go," I told Velvet. As I thanked her, I felt comforted by her aura of lavender, pink, and mystical greens—the colors of someone who's lived many times.

Then a memory hit me.

Old soul, Opal had said. Could she have meant Velvet?

"One more thing," I said quickly, opening my tote bag.

"What?" Velvet asked.

"Don't laugh, okay," I said, embarrassed. "But my spirit guide insisted I bring this along. I think she meant for me to show it to you. It's just a cheap toy."

I drew out the plastic, fake-jewel wand.

And Velvet didn't laugh.

She gasped.

"Heavens to the Goddess!" she cried, reeling back as her eyes grew wide. "It's Zathora's Muse!"

14

"Not the actual Muse," Velvet clarified as she reached out to touch the plastic wand, almost reverently. "But a duplicate that gives me chills considering its history. There's even the initial Z on the handle."

I followed her gaze to a tiny scratch of a "Z" I hadn't noticed before. "Who's Zathora?" I asked.

"A brilliant, eccentric, doomed soul." Velvet ran her fingers across the faux-jewels. "She died a century ago. In stage magician circles, her story is legend."

"Why?"

"Because she nearly achieved two amazing feats: bringing the dead back to life and breaking into the very male-dominated world of magicians." Velvet gave a wry chuckle. "Some say that the latter would have been the more amazing achievement. Being female and a magician was a rarity back then; come to think of it, even now it's uncommon. Can you name even one famous woman magician?"

I tried to think of one, but the only magicians I'd heard of were famous guys like Houdini, Copperfield, Blaine, and Angel.

Velvet's gaze was distant as she studied the wand. "It's strange that you would have a replica of the Muse. How did you get it?"

"It belongs to my friend Josh. He's apprenticed to the Amazing Arturo, so it's not unusual for him to have magic props. Why did you call this wand a muse?"

"Zathora claimed that her wand whispered the secrets of the universe to her, just like a muse inspires an artist to achieve greatness," Velvet explained. "At each performance, she would introduce her wand the way most magicians introduce their assistants."

"What happened to the real wand?"

"Buried with Zathora." Velvet pursed her lips thoughtfully. "From what I remember, the photos of the Muse showed amazing details, down to the circle of emeralds and sapphires near the tip—exactly like this one."

"These green and blue beads are plastic."

"Yes, they're not real, obviously, but this copy is extraordinary. Did Josh tell you anything about how he came to have it?"

"He doesn't know I have it. He left kind of abruptly and I took this to Thorn, hoping she could find him."

"And did she?"

"Well, she pointed to a large forested area on the map. But since then I've found out he's contacted his family and said he was okay."

"Yet you're still worried," Velvet guessed. "I'm sensing a connection between this wand and your young man."

"My *ex*-young man," I corrected. "And you're right, I am worried. It's silly, though, because he told his family he's safe. I just have this...I don't know...an uneasy feeling."

"Feelings can be messages from the other side." Velvet glanced down at the wand in her hand, frowning, then returning it to me. "You'll want to read up on Zathora."

Velvet led me into the back room, where candles flickered from wall sconces and heavy curtains blocked the bright daylight. She flicked on a light switch near a long bookshelf and ran her finger down titles. "Hmm, *The Experience of Magic* by Eugene Burger has fascinating information. It says that archeological evidence suggests the origin of the magic wand came from the lunar calendar stick, dating back 50,000 years."

"Wow, that's a long time ago."

She nodded, and I reached out my hand for the book, but she seemed to change her mind and instead gave me a different book. It was slimmer, with a silver and purple spine and a beautiful cover showing a woman with flowing silver hair. She was draped in a golden gown and surrounded by mystical stars, moons, and other symbols.

I read the title out loud: "*She-Magic.*"

"This one should have what you seek. It discusses the cosmic role of women who shaped the evolution of magic. There's a fascinating chapter on Zathora."

Confused but intrigued, I thanked Velvet and left with the book.

I planned to read it at home, but as soon as I got there my gaze fell on the barn, and a memory of Dominic's blue eyes overwhelmed me. A lump stuck in my throat. I stared, expecting to see a falcon soaring down from the high loft window or hear Dominic's voice calling my name. But I only heard chickens squawking and the soft roar of a wintry wind. Dark clouds were rolling in, darkening the sky.

I felt something brush my leg and looked down at Lilybelle, who was rubbing against my ankles. She meowed, and for a second my hopes rose.

"Is he back?" I whispered, bending down to pet her soft fur. "Did Dominic send you to get me?"

She meowed again, then ran up the porch steps and leaped for her favorite sitting spot on the rail. She curled up comfortably, and I took that as my answer.

And I died a little.

Moving slowly, my limbs heavy, I went inside and asked Nona if she'd heard anything. She knew what I meant without my saying it and simply shook her head.

I checked my phone (sitting by my computer instead of in my purse where it belonged) and found one missed call—from Manny. I didn't return his call. Instead, I covered myself in a warm quilt and curled up on the window seat in my room to read about She-Magic.

Skimming through, I learned that the role of women in the world of professional stage magicians was largely limited to being graceful, beautiful assistants. They bring props on and off stage, are the "victims" in tricks using torture devices, and often do most of the magic work while the male magician gets the applause.

There were also chapters about the few women magicians who did rise to fame and achievement. I read about Melinda Saxe, who was billed as "The First Lady of Magic" when she performed in Las Vegas; Dell O'Dell, who was considered one of the most successful female magicians of the twentieth century and had a TV show in the 1950s; and Clementine (AKA "Ionia the Enchantress"), who vanished from the stage when she became a princess.

Then I came to the chapter on Zathora.

She was born Jane Elizabeth Meade in 1894 and married a magician who mostly performed at local festivals. She worked as his assistant until a wire broke during a levitation trick and he fell to his death mid-performance. Jane renamed herself Zathora and struggled to work as a magician. The men who dominated the world of illusion excluded women from their secret magician societies. Women were rarely considered real magicians—until Zathora proclaimed she could bring the dead to life. When she revived small animals, usually birds or mice, on stage with no props other than her wand, audiences were bewitched. *Zathora the Miracle Maker,* they called her. She gained fame but still not the respect of male magicians, who called her *The Miracle Faker.*

So Zathora planned for the most amazing performance ever: she announced that she would kill herself on stage, then bring herself back to life.

When I turned to the next page, eager to find out what happened, there was a colored photo of Zathora with her Muse. A shudder rippled through me. I'd dreamed about this woman. Her copper hair rained down her slim shoulders and her smoldering eyes seemed to burn through the paper.

Reading on, I came to the last paragraph, which described how hundreds of people watched as Zathora literally died on stage. She swallowed a deadly poison and collapsed immediately. A doctor, waiting nearby, pronounced her dead. Then the hushed audience watched her still body, waiting for her to come back to life ... only she never did.

Rather than being the most famous woman magician in the world, she became a footnote of failures.

"So sad," I whispered as I closed the book. Still, it didn't explain why Josh had her faux-wand and why I'd dreamed about a woman who'd died nearly a century ago.

I picked up the Muse, turning it in my hand and watching the jewels blur their brilliant colors. I tried to tune in to the energy and envision the past or future. But unlike Thorn, who could follow a trail from a touch, I got nothing.

Setting both the book and the wand aside, I glanced at the clock. I felt like I'd lived a few lifetimes in the last couple of hours, yet it was barely noon. Usually the first day of winter vacation was cause for a celebration, like going to the mall with friends or taking my little sisters to a movie. But I had no plans. My sisters were in San Jose, Penny-Love was off with Thorn, and Dominic…

I sighed and left my room.

I wasn't really hungry, but eating was something to do. I poured kiwi-apple juice and sliced up left-over roast beef for a sandwich. I made one for Nona, too, since she was busy at her computer and sometimes forgot to eat if not reminded. As I set down her plate, my fingers brushed a folder titled *Heart Lights* and I wondered if she was serious about merging her business with Roger Aimsley's. My intuition triggered an image of a credit card bursting in flames. That couldn't be good.

But my intuition wasn't proof of anything, so I said nothing about my suspicions and went back upstairs to run a search on Mr. Heart Lights on my computer. I found a website with glowing reviews for his business. I tried a few different search engines but only came up with all kinds of positive comments. Everyone loved him, perhaps including Nona. So I had to trust her judgment.

I switched windows to catch up on my email. There were some jokes from my cheerleader pal Kaitlyn, a petition for a greener community from the other Catelyn, the usual spam, which I reported and deleted, and one message from my sister Ashley and nine from her twin, Amy.

Nothing from my third sister.

I heard the phone ring.

I didn't always get a name when I heard the phone, usually just a sense of age, gender, and the connection to me. So I knew it was a guy, someone from school. The energy felt warm, with pastel shades of trust and friendship seasoned with snappy purple attitude.

"Hey, Manny," I said as I picked up.

"Why didn't you call back? I've been waiting hours! Didn't you get my voicemail?" he demanded in an exaggerated, hurt tone. Manny could be such a drama king.

"Sorry, I forgot. Things have been all kinds of weird for me."

"Well, you are a weirdness magnet."

"I could do with less weirdness in my life." And more Dominic, I thought wistfully.

"Uh oh. What's wrong? You used the *tone.*"

"It's nothing ... much."

"Which means it's something...*lots*. Mystic Manny sees all and knows even more. He senses you are in great distress and invites you to dump your worries on his strong, muscular shoulders."

"How do you manage to make everything about you?"

"It's a god-given gift. I am humbled by my own magnificence."

I couldn't help but laugh, which felt strangely good. Maybe I just needed to let all my emotions out in a primal way, and laughing was better than screaming.

"So dump your crap on me," Manny said.

Debating how much to share, I held up my fingers on one hand and mentally counted my stress-issues:

1. Dominic probably headed to jail for murder, if he couldn't prove he'd acted in self-defense.

2. My half-sister missing after meeting a vandal.

3. My best friends conspiring to solve Jacques' murder.

Manny didn't know about #3, so I had to be careful not to let it slip. Also, I wasn't ready to talk about Dominic with anyone—it was too raw and painful. So I told him about Jade.

"Jade's missing?" Manny asked, surprised.

"Yeah—after she met with Grey."

"The same guy who Josh left with," Manny said, and I heard a jingle of beads so I knew he was shaking his beaded dreadlocks. "Is Jade interested in magicians, too?"

"Depends on how you mean that. Jade was interested in Grey, which is why she met with him. And get this— they met at Trick or Treats. The scene of his first crime."

"And now Jade is missing just like Josh." Manny sounded perplexed.

"Josh may not be missing," I told him. "He called home and said he'd be back by Christmas."

"How touching. But I bet he didn't tell his family where he was." Manny's tone hinted that he knew a secret.

I shrugged. "I don't know."

"Well I do." I could imagine the cocky grin on his face. "I did some checking on the Amazing Arturo, and let me tell you, he's one evasive dude. His website is all flash and no substance—like a magic trick where you think you see him but it's all an illusion. Arturo isn't even his name. The dude's birth name was Zacharius Arthur Pizowitz. And get this—he has a criminal record for theft and forging checks."

"Josh's mentor was in jail?" I gasped, standing up from my computer chair.

"Three years in a minimum security prison in his twenties. Then he got married and cleaned up his act." Manny chuckled. "That's a pun…act, performance. Get it?"

I groaned.

"His wife, Genevieve LaFleur, is loaded. She sugar-mommas his career. She even performs as his assistant, and I've seen a picture of her. She's really hot for her age, with curves where it counts if you know what I mean."

"I think I saw a photo of them at Josh's house." I heard the rustling of pages and imagined Manny flipping through his print-out. "What else did you find out?"

"Under Arturo's real name, he owns a long list of investments and real estate—including a cabin on two hundred acres in Sap Hollow."

"Where's that?"

"In the mountains."

I thought back to Thorn and the map. "Near Auburn?"

"Yeah. It's remote and hard to find—a secret compound for magicians. I checked for a satellite image and could only see a bit of roof, a lake, and shiny glints that could be cars. I'll send you the link and you can see for yourself. But don't waste your time trying to go there—it's surrounded in security fences. You'd never get inside."

"I don't plan to. Josh can take care of himself. I'm more worried about Jade—I'm afraid to guess what Grey did to her. My dad can't even track Grey down. If only I knew his last name."

"There are other ways of finding someone," Manny said. "Think hard. Tell me everything you know about him."

"Only that he's part of Arturo's magician group, he drives a blue Mustang convertible, and he smashes up candy shops for kicks."

"Double trouble boil and bubble," Manny said, completely messing up the actual *Macbeth* quote. "Have you tried asking your spirit guide for answers?"

"Opal pops in whenever she wants, not when I want her to."

"Can't hurt to try. She's helped you before."

"Lately she's been more confusing than usual. It would be easier to—" A beep interrupted me.

I glanced at Caller ID: *Unknown Number.* Probably a telemarketer, I thought, and I was going to ignore the call until I got a strong feeling—like a fingernail jabbing me in the psyche—that urged me to answer. So I told Manny I had to go and clicked over to the new call.

I heard a familiar voice.

And I gasped.

"Jade!" I clung to the phone like it would vanish if I let go.

"Yeah, it's me," whispered my half-sister.

"Ohmygod! I can hardly believe you're calling!" I babbled. "Where are you? Why did you go off with Grey? You know he's bad news, after what he did to Trick or Treats. Are you flipping crazy?"

"Shut up, Sabine. No time to go into all that."

I bit my lip to hold my temper. "Just tell me if you're okay."

"Yeah, but scary stuff could happen if they catch me on the phone. This room is off-limits—especially to me."

"What room? Where are you?"

"With the magicians. I'll explain when I see you."

"You're coming here?"

"I wish! But they won't let me leave!" Her voice was shrill with panic. "They're always watching and only let me out once a day for a noon walk—like a dog!"

"You mean you're a prisoner?" I exclaimed in disbelief.

"Yeah."

"So call 911!"

"I can't, and you better not either. You can't tell any-one! I mean it, Sabine. Or Grey will kill Josh."

"Grey hurt Josh? But that's crazy! They're friends!"

"Not so much," she said bitterly. "Grey is one sick dude."

"I don't understand any of this." I spun the chair away from the computer and, with one hand pressing the phone to my ear, I picked up the faux wand from my dresser. I ran my fingertips over the colorful jewels, closing my eyes and trying to see past the plastic but getting nothing. "So why did you go with Grey?" I asked Jade.

"To find Josh."

"Last time we talked, you didn't sound worried about him." And you betrayed me, I thought bitterly.

"I wasn't, but I knew you were, so I decided to find him for you."

"Why?"

"To make up for being such a bitch."

"An apology would have been easier."

"Not when you won't answer your damned phone," Jade retorted. "Why didn't you call me back?"

"I was too angry and..." Emotions cracked my voice. "It's bad enough that you're going out with Evan, but trash talking me hurt."

"Maybe it did, but you weren't the only one hurt. You said stuff to me too. But I was willing to drop my pride and admit I was sorry. Only you never gave me a chance. Then after I left Evan's, I stopped for gas and there was Josh's pal Grey filling up his convertible. I caught him checking me out like he knew me."

"Probably because you look like me."

"You look like *me,*" she corrected in a superior I'm-older-than-you way. "Anyway, that's when I came up with the idea to find Josh. So I sweet-talked Grey, then let him think I was into bad-ass guys like him. I even admitted I knew what he'd done at Trick or Treats and thought it was cool."

"Cool?" I choked with outrage. "More like horrible."

"I was playing him and saying what I thought he wanted to hear. It worked, too, and I could tell he was really into me. When I asked about Josh, he said, 'He's exactly where I want him.' I got a bad feeling and was more determined to find Josh. So I told Grey he didn't have the guts to go back to Trick or Treats and I dared him to meet me there."

"But why? That doesn't make any sense."

"It would have if you'd answered my calls," she snapped. "I thought you could spy on our meeting and when Grey left, you could follow him to Josh. And that turned out well—*not*. So I convinced him to let me go with him, and now I'm trapped in a cult of crazies and Josh is locked up until the initiation."

"Initiation?" The word sent tremors through me.

"Yeah—no clue what that's about. Everyone is dressed weird and talks strange and I swear I saw a head floating by itself. I want out of here ASAP! I'm afraid that—" She cut off abruptly. "I hear footsteps! Listen fast. I'm in the mountains at the freaky magician retreat owned by the Amazing—"

"Arturo," I finished.

"Do you know how to get here?"

"I can find out."

"Good! That will make it easier for you to—" Jade gasped. "Someone's at the door! Sabine, come be me tomorrow! Noon. Damn!"

The phone went dead.

*   *   *

Years seemed to pass as I stared at the phone, stunned.

The temptation to call Jade back was overwhelming,

but I knew in my gut she wouldn't—*couldn't*—answer. And what if someone else answered? Jade, and Josh, could end up in worse trouble. Jade's words played over and over in my head, spreading fear like a raging wildfire.

Would Grey really kill Josh?

I remembered the destruction Grey left at Trick or Treats after he'd smashed the glass candy cases with the bat. Someone that violent was capable of anything. But Josh was his friend, so why would Grey threaten him? And why on earth kidnap Jade?

I mentally listed all the weird stuff in sequence:

- Josh going off with Arturo—totally out of character.
- Jade hooking up with Evan—combusting into an epic argument.
- Jade playing Nancy Drew, setting up the meeting with Grey. Disaster!

Had Jade really done that to help me? Or was it some kind of rivalry? She'd spent the last four years, even before I knew she existed, trying to be like me (better than me?) by copying my interests (school newspaper and fencing). What did she hope to prove? And who did she want to impress?

This wasn't the time to go all pseudo-therapist. Jade was a prisoner and counting on me to help her. Josh was in danger, too. Had Grey forced Josh to call his parents, so they wouldn't report him missing? Was the magician society some kind of warped cult that tortured its new members?

The dial tone droned and I realized I was still holding the phone. Flipping it closed, I paced my room. I wanted to rush to the rescue, bringing Jade and Josh back ASAP. Of course, going alone would be all kinds of stupid.

But Jade had been adamant: we couldn't tell anyone. Besides, what would I say? "Excuse me, Officer, but my half-sister and ex-boyfriend are being held prisoner in the mountains by professional stage magicians." The Amazing Arturo was highly respected. Adults wouldn't believe a teen over him without convincing evidence. And Josh's parents hadn't reported him missing, thinking he was safe with his mentor.

Even as I debated this, I knew I was going to go rescue them. But I wouldn't be stupid about it—I'd let someone know where I was going. Only who?

Definitely not my father. He'd order me to stay at home, then he'd call the police.

Nona wouldn't want me to go after Jade either, and she might call Dad.

I couldn't involve Penny-Love or Thorn—they already had too much drama.

What about Manny? I could trust him with my secrets, but what if he got all macho and wanted to come with me? He had superhero powers with a computer ... but he wasn't so great in the wild outdoors.

My gaze drifted out my window to the barn...the empty loft room. There was only one person I wanted to turn to. Dominic would know what to do, but he hadn't even called.

Flopping on my bed and curling a pillow under my head, I stared up at the ceiling, tracing ideas in the paint swirls. After tossing out all the things I couldn't do, I still needed to let someone know where I was going, just in case I needed backup, and Manny was my choice. I'd text him—but not until I was far enough away that he couldn't come after me. I'd send the text once I reached the retreat.

Before I did anything drastic, though, I'd write down everything Jade told me so I wouldn't forget. I'd been so shocked to hear her voice that our conversation was a blur. It took an hour to write down words and phrases from my memory, and even then I wasn't sure if I had it down verbatim. What had Jade said before we were disconnected?

Come meet me tomorrow?

Close but not quite right.

Come be me tomorrow.

Yeah, that's what she said—cryptic and abbreviated, sort of like a verbal text. What was she trying to say? Probably something like, "Come be with me at Arturo's mountain retreat tomorrow."

But Arturo's retreat was on a hundred wooded acres. How could I find her?

Think, I urged myself. Had Jade given me any other clues?

I looked at my notes again. Jade said she went out every day at noon for a walk "like a dog." And before hanging up, she'd said I should be there at noon.

So all I had to do was:

1. Drive to Arturo's hideaway.
2. Sneak past any security fences.
3. Find a walking trail.
4. Rescue Jade.

But if Jade couldn't get off the property, how was I supposed to get in? And what about Josh? I had to rescue him. I couldn't leave him with a "friend" who might kill him.

Something about Jade's message still didn't feel right—I had the sense that I'd jumped to the wrong conclusion and overlooked an important piece of information. Glancing down at my paper again, I analyzed each word. But it was the missing words—the ones I'd had to guess at—that nagged at me.

Reading through it one more time, I suddenly understood.

Jade *had* told me her plan—an extreme, crazy plan. It'd never work, but it couldn't hurt to try.

I knew where to go now: the mall.

I was going shopping.

16

The mall on the last Saturday before Christmas was insane.

After years of searching for a parking space, I made my way through an obstacle course of frenzied shoppers into a burst of climate-controlled warm air. The cacophony of voices and holiday music rattled my brain so much it was hard to think—which wasn't a bad thing, because if I thought too much I'd lose my nerve.

I noticed two guys and a girl from school, loaded with shopping bags. The girl smiled and waved. I waved back, but couldn't smile. Hanging out at the mall was usually fun, but being here alone was sad and ironic. Penny-Love and I had planned to come here before life changed drastically. All the awful drama with Jacques and Jade and Josh.

How strange to be here without any friends, passing jewelry shops advertising 75 percent off diamonds, a bath and body shop with an elf offering free soap samples, a toy store with singing electronic snowmen. I felt disconnected, as if the silver cord connecting me to ordinary life had been severed.

Wheels squealed and I jumped aside to avoid getting rolled over by a young mom pushing a stroller. She didn't pause or apologize. Why were some people so rude? I hurried along, pausing at a Hallmark shop, a favorite of Penny-Love's. She thought it was hilarious to read the goofy rhymes on romantic cards. A few times she even invented her own corny rhymes and turned them into cheers, jumping and chanting without caring if anyone was watching.

So where was Penny-Love right now? Still in shock over finding Jacques' body? And had Thorn been serious about finding Jacques' murderer for her? I hoped not— that was just too dangerous. But they'd missed the last few days of school, so something must be up. What was going on with my friends?

There was one way to find out.

I sat down on a bench by a play area where little kids

squealed as they climbed ropes and slid down slides. Then I pulled out my cell.

"Hey, Sabine," Penny-Love answered casually. Like she hadn't been splattered in blood and mourning her dead boyfriend less than a week ago.

"Pen, are you okay?" I exclaimed, bending over to muffle my voice.

"Sure. Why wouldn't I be?"

"Last time I saw you, you were in bad shape. What's been going on?"

She groaned. "Too much to explain. Can this wait till I get back?"

"No, it can not. Get back? Where are you?"

"Bakersfield."

"You did *not* just say Bakersfield!"

"Crazy, huh?" Penny-Love's laugh was brittle.

"Talk fast and tell me everything. How did you get to Bakersfield?"

"In Thorn's car. Actually, it's her mother's jeep and a sick shade of yellow. It took like four hours to get here. That's why we missed school—not that there's anything important at school before a vacation. Everything happened too fast, and we had to keep going or lose the guy."

"What guy?"

"The dude sneaking out of Jacques' apartment. When we were staking it out, this chunky guy with sideburns—totally not a good look for him, by the way—came out carrying boxes. So Thorn said, 'Let's follow him.' I said, 'Don't be stupid.' But you know how she never listens to me. The guy got on the freeway and headed south. We almost lost him when we had to stop for gas in Fresno, but Thorn can drive really fast."

"Let me get this straight." I switched the phone to my other ear, as if maybe that would somehow clear up this crazy conversation. "You followed a stranger—possibly a murderer—all the way to Bakersfield and you're still there?"

"Still here." Huge sigh. "Totally bored in the car while Thorn does who-knows-what in a library. She said I'd just get in the way and ordered me to wait here. She can really piss me off! Like on the drive down, after I drank this huge cup of Pepsi, she wouldn't stop for a bathroom and I had to hold it for like two hours. When we finally stopped, we found out something totally shocking."

"I can't take any more shocks today," I said, thinking about Jade.

"Then I hope you're sitting down. The guy we were fol-lowing—" Penny-Love paused dramatically. "He's a cop!"

"A *cop!*" I spoke so loudly that a father holding a sleep-ing baby glared at me.

"He switched into his uniform at the memorial ser-vice he was headed to. Thorn and I went too, since it was crowded and we figured no one would notice. It was for a thirty-one-year-old rookie detective named Oscar Dalton. We listened while the cop talked about how badly Oscar would be missed, and how his death during a drug-deal-gone-wrong was senseless. It was so sad, listening to Oscar's parents and his fiancée."

"Whoa! That's a lot to take in—cops, funeral, drugs. But how does this fit in with everything?" I grimaced, wondering about the gun Thorn had hidden.

"Well, that's how we found out Jacques was a big fat cheating liar. 'Course, we had no idea we'd find this out hundreds of miles from home, at his funeral."

"What?"

"You heard me." Penny-Love paused in a familiar drama-girl way. "Oscar and Jacques were the same person."

"But you said Oscar was thirty-one and engaged!"

"Jacques wasn't his real name—he was working undercover."

"At our school?" I watched a little kid hanging on a bar by his knees, my thoughts turned upside-down, too. "No way!"

"Everything about my so-called boyfriend was fake. He was a big fat cheating liar. Oh … here's Thorn." I heard a shuffling sound and muffled voices.

"Hey, Sabine," Thorn cut in, an edge to her voice that fit the barbed-wire jewelry she usually wore. "So did Pen fill you in?"

"I'm still tripping on Jacques being a cop," I admitted.

"A NARC," Thorn said bluntly. "That's why his death wasn't reported. Jacques never existed. Officer Oscar Dal-

177

ton died while working undercover. No one would say much more than that—except that he wasn't shot. He was stabbed."

"Stabbed? But what about the gun!"

The dad nearest to me snatched up his baby and glared daggers at me again, then strode away from the play area.

"I think the gun was Oscar's," Thorn guessed. "He must have grabbed it to defend himself, only the other guy was faster. I don't know much—but seeing his friends and family made it more real ... and sad."

Her tone was heavy, and I felt sad, too. A life was lost. No matter how or why, he'd been someone we knew, and he had family and friends who mourned him. Still, I wondered why a NARC had chosen Penny-Love as a girlfriend. Had he thought she had drug connections because she was mega-popular? Maybe her hyper personality made him assume she was a druggie. Of course, he would have quickly figured out he was wrong. So why didn't he dump her?

Oh yeah ... he *did* dump her.

"Are you and Pen coming home now?" I asked Thorn. "It sounds like we're all off the hook."

"Except we still hid his gun, and I want to find out more about that folder with Josh's photo on it. I have a weird feeling it's important."

Now that she mentioned the folder, I had the same feeling.

"Do you know where it is?" I asked her.

"Probably in one of the boxes that the cop took from Jacques' apartment."

"The box could be anywhere by now. How can you find it?"

She chuckled. "How do I find anything?"

I was smiling as I closed my phone until I glanced up at the dad-with-baby, who was having a whispered conversation with a mall security cop and pointing my way.

My cue to exit.

I checked the store directory, found the specialty store that I hoped would have what I needed, then made my way up an escalator to the second floor. It was just as crazy-crowded here, and I had to move quickly or risk being knocked over.

I stopped at a shop with a window display showing a pirate, a Klingon, and a unicorn. This was the place.

When I left the mall an hour later, my arms were sagging with bags. My trusty credit card had gotten a good workout. Fortunately, my parents expected me to splurge on Christmas gifts. There was no reason to explain that my purchases had nothing to do with the holiday.

For the rest of the day I was a bundle of nerves. Nona had lunched with Mr. Heart Lights again and was so excited about the prospect of merging professionally (and romantically?) that she didn't pay much attention to me. I was too worried to eat much at dinner, shifting my food on my plate while I tapped my fingernails on the table and pretended to listen to my grandmother. When she asked if I was okay, I lied and said, "Great." But she studied me, her psychic radar sweeping over me, and I could tell she was suspicious.

I hated lying to my grandmother, but sometimes it was necessary.

Unfortunately, one lie snowballed into more, and the next day I came up with a story about meeting Penny-Love and Thorn at the Roseville Galleria. It was such a huge, busy mall, and the drive there so long, that Nona wouldn't expect me to return for hours.

I just hoped I returned, period.

I prepared a backpack full of emergency supplies like snacks, a flashlight, a multi-use knife, water bottles, a first-aid kit, and at the last minute I'd tossed in Josh's plastic Muse wand. For luck, I wore the charm bracelet that had belonged to my great, great, etc. grandmother. The tiny silver fish, house, cat, and book dangled from my wrist, catching the light as I drove up Highway 80 past Roseville. I followed the signs for Auburn.

Crossing my fingers, I hoped my plan would go smoothly and that by evening, Jade and Josh would be home. Safe.

The towering trees bordering the road like warrior guards gave me a scary feeling—it seemed like I was winding farther and farther away from reality. The trees stretched so tall that their piney needles prickled the sky and shut out the sun. This was a startling contrast to yesterday's bustling mall.

I felt as if I was leaving humanity and entering a strange landscape of endless trees.

I followed the directions Manny had sent me, and left the main highway for a narrow, paved road that wound deeper into the forest. Although it seemed completely remote here, I noticed signs and steep roads that disappeared down the hillsides. I checked the address for Arturo's property again: 1022 Sap Tree Road. I drove slower, and still almost missed the turn for Sap Tree.

Once I was on that road, I had to look among bushes and trees for markers or mailboxes. There weren't many and they were spaced miles apart: 1005, 1013, 1019. The numbers ended when I passed a beautiful lake in a deep canyon, glittering like a jewel in the sun. I kept going, relieved when I found some numbered signs again. But wait a minute—the numbers resumed at 1115.

How had I missed Arturo's address?

Spinning a three-point turn in a wide spot in the road, I drove back. I passed the lake again, noting a sail boat drifting toward a towering man-made dam.

But I kept my gaze firmly on the side of the road— until I saw a skinny wood marker with engraved numbers: 1022. But where was the driveway to this address? I pulled over, and had to step out and peer under an umbrella of trees before I saw faint tracks in the dirt leading to a big metal gate.

Cautiously, I moved closer to the gate, noticing a camera attached to the top of it like an alien eyeball. And on each side of the entryway, signs warned:

KEEP OUT! PRIVATE!
TRESPASSERS WILL BE ELECTROCUTED!

Electrocuted? I gulped. I heard a low buzz of wires and realized they were charged with electricity. Way extreme security! What were Arturo and his magician pals hiding?

When the alien eye swiveled in my direction, I hustled back into the car and locked the doors. Then I drummed my fingers on the wheel and thought hard. I couldn't enter at the gate or bust through the electric fence—which seemed to go on for miles, probably all around the lake. Yet there had to be some way to get in without being electrocuted. But even if I found an entrance, it would take serious hiking equipment and skills to search the steep terrain.

Since I wasn't accomplishing anything here, I reversed the car and drove slowly down the road, following the silver flash of fencing. Then I saw it—a dented section, as if a car had lost control and smashed into it. The damage wasn't that obvious unless you were looking closely.

Pulling my car off the road, I looked for warnings about electricity here but found none. When I bent down to peer at the dented section, I saw what I was hoping for—a jagged rip just big enough for a person to squeeze through. And beyond the fence I spotted a rugged path, probably created by wild animals. The path plunged down to the glittering blue lake at the canyon's bottom. This wasn't a natural lake, but a huge body of water held back by a gleaming white dam. Silver-gray rocks avalanched down to the sparkling water, and on the opposite end of the lake, small boats bobbed by a long narrow pier. On the shore there were clusters of dark shapes that I guessed were cabins.

I casually looked around to make sure I was completely alone, then jumped back into my car. I quickly sent Manny a text, letting him know where I was, then parked the car so that it was half-hidden under the thick foliage. I took my charm bracelet off and tucked it safely in my backpack, then shoved my backpack through the rip in the fence and started squeezing myself through after it. The hole was big enough for squirrels but a tight fit for me. Still, I squirmed and dug at the soft red dirt until my head was through the opening, then my shoulders, hips, and . . .

I was on the other side!

"Woo hoo!" I did a little happy dance, dusting off dirt and shaking a twig out of my hair. I slipped the backpack over my shoulders and sucked in a deep breath, my triumph fading as I realized the true steepness of the path. It was a long way down to the lake, and looked like a rough hike through the dense foliage. It would be a treacherous fall if I lost my balance.

Cautiously, I hugged the craggy embankment, pushing aside weeds and sometimes crawling to get through the prickly branches. Taking one step at a time, I balanced with the caution of a tightrope walker. Then gravel rolled under my shoes, and I grabbed a tree trunk before falling flat on my butt. I heard a rip but I kept moving, going deeper into the rugged woods. And then the ground leveled out a bit and I reached the edge of the dam. It wasn't a thin wall, like I'd expected, but a thick mountain of gravel and concrete.

Jade was probably across the lake, near where I'd spotted the cabins and boats. There would be trails, and the brush wouldn't be as thick that close to the water. As long as I didn't run into any electric fences, it shouldn't be too hard to follow the edge of the lake.

But I couldn't go anywhere looking like this. Frowning down at my dirt-caked clothes, I was really glad I'd brought other clothes. And they were more than just any clothes, in fact. I smiled a little as I took off my backpack and pulled out a pair of white-washed designer jeans and a glitzy gold bag, which held a few special items and cosmetics.

There was only one thing left to complete my new look.

I pulled out a long, wavy, red wig.

17

Peering into my hand mirror was like a magic trick: now you see Sabine, now you don't. It was my own face, but when framed with crimson curls and bangs, reality shifted so that I could see Jade too. It was as if we were double-exposed into one image.

I was certain that Jade had literally meant: Come. Be. Me.

And we *did* look alike. All I'd needed was a long red wig, a cerulean blue shirt to mute the green in my eyes, and a hippy sway when I strutted in my new skinny-ass jeans. I'd layered on a wool-lined brown jacket, too, since the mountains were chilly. Being Jade would make me less conspicuous if anyone saw me, especially from a distance. Still, it felt weird to have fiery-red curls instead of straight blond hair tumbling down my shoulders.

Moving away from the dam, I followed a rough path through brush. It curved and dipped along the cliff edge high above the shoreline, then plunged into a pine-scented forest of spiraling needles and lacy leaves, which swallowed me. Although the sun was shining somewhere far above me, the temperature dropped so that my breath was a foggy puff and a chill shivered through my jacket. Fallen leaves crackled beneath my feet and I kicked pine cones away. When I started to slip on a patch of ice, I dug my heels in to catch myself, glad I'd opted for sturdy leather ankle boots rather than fashion-worthy high heels.

Just when I was beginning to wonder if I'd ever reach anything close to civilization, the drapery of leafy green around me shifted, offering a glimpse of the cabins.

Is that where I'd find a walking trail that would lead to Jade?

My heart fluttered like the dark birds flitting above me in the tangled branches. When a larger bird with scarlet-brown wings swooped toward me, my hope soared and I thought it was Dagger. But it wasn't a falcon, just a red-tailed hawk.

It was stupid to imagine Dominic being close by, I scolded myself. I couldn't let myself think about him ... about the hours we spent in the tree house, laughing at squirrels and playing card games ... and holding each other, so very close. God, how I missed him.

But hope ran deep. Maybe I should just try calling him, even though I was sure he wouldn't—couldn't—answer. I flipped my phone open ... then groaned. Not even one signal bar. I couldn't call anyone! Not Dominic, Manny, Penny-Love, Thorn, Nona, or 911. I'd have to return to the road to get a signal. But it was already past eleven o'clock, so either I kept searching for Jade or turned back now.

Not a quitter, I kept going.

When the trail started to twist deeper into the forest, veering away from the cabins rather than toward them, I wondered if I should double back. Had I missed a path? I began to seriously doubt my plan. What had I been think-ing? Coming here alone, dressing up like Jade, and now headed for who-knows-where? What if I'd completely got-ten Jade's message wrong and was trespassing on the wrong property?

Biting my lip, I pivoted slowly in the circle of massive, sky-blocking trees. Pine needles shivered in the wind and a gray squirrel skittered across the branches. Life pulsed around me in gold, green, and tawny auras, welcoming yet warning of hidden dangers. I considered retreating, feeling small and lost in this vast jungle of woods. Instead, I gritted my teeth, determined, sinking deeper and darker into the forest shadows. Within five minutes, the trees curved overhead like a dark tunnel and shut out the sun, blanketing me in chilly grayness.

But I kept going, holding the image of blue water in my mind. And in a startling instant, I came out in a sunny meadow with a sweeping view of the dancing azure waters.

Four cabins zoomed into view: square wooden structures no bigger than my bedroom at home, crafted with rugged logs. It was as if I'd slipped back in time a few centuries. There was no sign of people or a walking trail. And it was almost noon.

So where was Jade? Trapped inside one of those cabins?

Fear pushed me faster until I was running down the path. But then I stopped because, out of the corner of my eye, I caught movement—not from the cabins, but back by the dam where I'd started this insane trek. Cupping my hand over my eyes, I stared at the dam, figuring the flash of movement must have been an animal. But instead I saw four shapes—and only one moved on four legs. The other three were definitely human, and they were crossing the dam like it was a bridge.

Or a walking trail?

Jade had said: "Come be me. Noon. Damn!" I'd assumed the "damn" was because she had been caught sneaking a phone call. But what if her final word had been "dam," a direction clue? Although it was hard to tell from so far away, one of the walkers either wore a red hat or had red hair.

Just great, I thought, twisting a curl of faux-red hair around my finger. I'd spent nearly an hour hiking *away* from the dam. Now I'd have to go all the way back.

Hiking uphill was killer. I stopped to rest midway, bending and panting for breath as I leaned against my knees. On the ground, oval and half-moon-shaped paw prints clawed the path. I wondered what animals had made them. Once, on a walk, Dominic had taught me how to identify different animal tracks. Raccoon, deer, foxes, possums, bobcats. We'd compared our own footprints, laughing a little at how his shoe was nearly twice the size of mine. Then we'd compared our hands, mine slipping into his as if they were made for each other.

Thoughts of Dominic were like sharp claws ripping at my heart. Where was he now? Was he in jail? Sometimes I could mentally reach out to Dominic, as if my soul slipped beside his, sharing thoughts and emotions. But now I felt ... nothing. Abandoned, disconnected, alone.

Desperate, I reached out for my spirit guide. Opal often said she was always close by. Closing my eyes, I tried summoning her, and I did sense something: a whisper of energy, subtle as a butterfly's flutter. Yet she didn't show herself, only whispered a faint *Keep going*.

So I did ... but it was *not* easy. As the trail narrowed, branches snatched like vicious claws at my clothes and wig.

I slapped, ducked, side-stepped, and even had to get down on my knees and crawl through a narrow opening in the branches.

Hurry, I told myself, my urgency growing.

Brittle twigs crunched under my boots. I stumbled over a jagged stone, but caught myself by grabbing a hanging branch. Then the forest rose up and I was back on the narrow cliff path leading to the dam. Like castle battlements, the silvery-gray dam rose out of the sparkling water and spread horizontally. And the top of the dam was in fact a paved road, wide enough for a parade.

And indeed it looked like a parade, when the group came closer.

Three people and a giant poodle.

The poodle was midnight black with curly fur, a standard poodle, and was tugging impatiently on his leash, dragging a stocky, middle-aged man whose blue cape plumed behind him. Next came an older man, walking with a cane that seemed more like a prop. He reminded me of a #2 pencil—tall and thin with a tuff of scruffy orange hair. And trailing after him was a redheaded girl...

JADE!

I started to call out to her, then stopped myself. Hadn't she told me she was a prisoner? Although her companions didn't look dangerous, I didn't want them to see me—and they were headed this way.

Ducking underneath a canopy of trees, I wondered

how I could get to Jade without the others seeing me. At their leisurely pace, they'd pass by my hiding place in about fifteen minutes. What I needed was a diversion, so I could contact Jade without alerting Blue Cape and Cane Man.

While I was crouched down trying to come up with a plan, Jade beat me to it by stumbling into Cane Man. It was not an accident, I could tell.

The elderly man cried out, his arms flailing, and dropped his cane. It tumbled and rolled toward the dam's steep graveled embankment. When he grabbed for it, he bumped into Blue Cape, who stumbled and lost his grip on the dog's leash.

The energetic poodle took off.

"I'll get him!" Jade's voice drifted down the dam and across the water. Then she sprinted away from them and down the trail toward my hiding place.

I ran to intercept her, imagining how grateful she'd be to see me. She'd cry for joy and thank me for rescuing her. She might even hug me, and I'd hug her back in a mature I-forgive-you-for-being-a-bitch way. Then we'd escape together.

Unfortunately, the poodle was faster than Jade. I don't know if he smelled me or if I was just in his way, but before I could move aside, he pounced on me.

"Get off!" I pushed him away.

The dog barked, then slurped at my face with his long slobbering tongue.

"He won't hurt you but his dog breath can be lethal."

"Jade!" I rolled away from the poodle, then jumped up and rushed to my half-sister. I opened my arms, inviting a hug, but she held back.

"Hey, Sabine." She shrugged like we were meeting casually at a mall instead of in the wilderness. "So you came."

"That was the plan, right?"

"Yeah, but I didn't think you'd figure it out."

Furious retorts jumped into my head, but I was too weary for arguments. "Well, I'm here, and I even did all this so I'd look like you." I gestured at my get-up.

"Lime-green eye shadow?" Jade rolled her eyes. "You'd never fool anyone who knows me. The wig is too curly, and you're smaller up there."

I clenched my teeth. "How about you *not* insult me?"

"Just saying my opinion." Her expression softened. "You know, I have lots of friends at school, but none of them would have done this for me. You got my brand of jeans right and the wig isn't terrible."

"You're welcome."

"Whatever." She smiled wryly. "I'm glad you're here."

"It wasn't easy finding this place—and even harder getting inside."

"But you never give up and you always figure things out. Dependable, considerate, clever Sabine. Just ask Dad. He says I'm too undisciplined and he wants me to be more like you."

I stared at her, shocked. "No way."

"He brags about how you help out your grandmother, get good grades, and go out with a great guy."

"The great guy broke up with me. I'm not sure what my parents will think of Dominic, but that could be interesting." I grinned. "If it makes you feel better, Dad shows he cares by lecturing. Trust me—he's not a fan of everything I do. When it comes to my psychic stuff, he has this 'don't ask, don't tell' policy. And he lectures me about how I should be more like my little sisters."

"Well, they are cute," Jade said, grinning wickedly.

"And they never get into trouble."

"Like we do," Jade teased.

"Let's avoid trouble this time by getting Josh and leaving ASAP," I said with a worried look up at the dam. Cane Man was reaching over the dam embankment, trying to grab his cane, but there was no sign of Blue Cape.

"We can't get Josh," she replied.

"What do you mean? Josh is the reason we both came here and I'm not leaving without him."

"I'm glad you feel that way," Jade said with a secretive smile.

I glanced over at the dam again. "Let's get moving! Your friends will reach us soon."

"You think they're my friends? I'm seriously insulted. I only walk with them to get outside. Otherwise I'm trapped inside all day."

"We'll both be trapped if we don't hustle." I grabbed her arm, but she pulled back and frowned at me.

"Wait. I have to tell you something."

"Tell me all about it while we walk."

"But I can't... I mean ... You need to know—"

"All I need to know is where Josh is." Spidery red curls brushed across my mouth and I slapped them away. "I can't wait to take this itchy thing off."

"Don't!" Jade protested, jerking my arm. "Keep it on."

"Why?"

"Because it's safer."

"The only safe thing is to get moving... oh!" Something nudged my ankle and I instinctively jumped back, just as the black poodle hiked his leg.

"No, Roscoe!" Jade grabbed the poodle's collar, tugging him away.

"I'm not a tree." He wagged his tail as if I'd patted his head instead of criticized him. "Tie him up so he won't follow us and ruin everything."

"He's the least of our worries," Jade said ominously as she glanced over her shoulder. Up on the dam, Blue Cape was helping Cane Man retrieve his cane. "Where's your car parked?"

"On the road past the dam." I pointed.

She nodded, her brows knitted as if thinking hard. "Did you bring a phone?"

"In my backpack. But there's no reception with all

these pine trees. Jade, could you stop asking questions and tell me where Josh is?"

"We can't both leave." She stared down at the dirt path, then back at me, frowning.

"What's your problem?" I folded my arms across my chest. "I went to a lot of trouble to come here—to rescue you guys—and now you don't want to leave!"

"It's complicated." Jade ran her fingers through her tangled hair. "I need to be here till tomorrow night for the Solstice ceremony."

"What ceremony?"

She shook her head. "I'm so sorry."

"Sorry about wh—"

Jade shut me down by lifting her head and shouting out toward the dam, "OVER HERE! I HAVE ROSCOE!"

A man shouted back, "Jade! I'm coming!"

"WAIT! I'LL BRING HIM TO YOU!" Jade yelled.

I glared at my half-sister. "Are you out of your mind? Why did you do that?"

She stepped away from me, not meeting my gaze.

"Jade, we've got to get moving *now*. Tie the dog to a tree."

"Don't you get it?" Jade actually had tears in her eyes as she whirled around to face me. "Grey threatened to kill Josh if I left before Solstice. I know you broke up with Josh, but do you want him to die?"

"Of course not! I came to help you both escape."

"I know … and thanks. I've seen what Grey can do … and he's beyond cruel." Jade closed her eyes, shuddering. Then she took a deep breath, as if cleansing a horrible memory. "After we got here, Grey let on that he thought it would be a fun thing for me to be his magician's assistant. Since I wanted to find Josh, I played along, flirting. I was dumb enough to think his bad-boy attitude was hot. But he persuaded me"—she grimaced—"to assist him with magic acts where he did cruel things to animals … and even to me." She took off her leather jacket and showed me strange jagged cuts on her arm. "He likes to play with knives."

Knives? I remembered Penny-Love and Thorn saying that Jacques had been stabbed. Could Grey have anything to do with it? And there was also my vision of Josh stabbing himself. This was not looking good.

"Oh, Jade." I reached out to hug her. "I'm so sorry you had to go through that. But that only proves how we really need to get going. *Now.*"

"Just listen, okay? You need to understand that I came here with Grey because I imagined myself as a hero, bringing Josh home when you couldn't. But it turns out I'm not very brave. And I'm worried about Mom, too. What if she's gone off on another gambling binge since I'm not there to make her go to her Gamblers Anonymous meeting? I watch our money and pay all the bills. Don't you see, Sabine? I need to check on Mom, but if I leave now, Grey will go psycho-slasher on Josh."

"So let's get Josh and we'll all go together."

"Josh is locked up."

"Then we'll break him out!"

"Don't you think I've tried? But it's impossible—until after the ceremony."

I shivered. "What ceremony?"

"There's no time to go into that. But you're right. If Josh doesn't leave, he could get hurt."

"Why do you even care about Josh?" I asked. "You barely know him."

"Weird, huh? I'm losing my edge." Jade gave a grim laugh. "I'm impressed that Josh does magic tricks at hospitals for sick kids. He's one of the good guys—and I've dated enough jerks to know the good ones are rare, like an endangered species. I don't want anything to happen to him."

"Neither do I. But if we can't get him out now, we'll leave and bring back help. We'll tell the police or Dad."

"Can they move faster than Grey's knives?"

My breath caught as I remembered my vision of Josh in a rustic building wearing strange, old-fashioned clothes—similar to what Blue Cape was wearing—and stabbing a knife into his chest. My visions weren't always literal, but usually they held prophetic meaning. I'd learned to pay attention ... or regret it later.

"Okay, Jade," I said. "What should we do?"

"Trade jackets with me."

Her tone was forceful yet scared, too. I didn't understand or like it, but I did as she asked.

As Jade fastened my jacket closed, she pointed to my backpack. "What's in there?"

"Cell phone, keys, bottled water, snacks, other stuff we might need."

"Good prep."

"Jade, what are you thinking?"

"You already know, or you wouldn't be wearing a red wig." Her words were light, but her expression was dark enough to eclipse the sun. "Be me a little longer...please."

I stared at her. "I thought I was supposed to dress like this to sneak in, in case someone saw me." My heart sank as I noticed that even our boots matched.

She skewered me with a sharp look. "Do you want to help Josh?"

"Of course I do!"

"Then find him and convince him to leave," she insisted. "I'll only be a few hours—long enough to check on Mom. I'll send help back for you and Josh."

Before I could argue, Jade shoved the dog's leash into my hand and slung my backpack over her shoulder. Then she fled into the woods.

And vanished.

18

I clung to Roscoe's leash, too stunned to react.

Jade's "let's trade places" plan was crazy in so many ways I could hardly believe it was really happening—and I'd agreed to it! I didn't know anything about what she'd been doing this past week. Looking like her might fool some people, but when I didn't know someone's name or got lost trying to find a bathroom, suspicions would rise.

Bury me now, because I was *sooo* dead.

A shrill cry and pounding footsteps made me whirl

around. A blur of blue was lunging down the path directly toward me. Crying out, I tossed the leash aside and stumbled backwards, shielding my face with my arms.

A blue cape flapped behind the running man like he was a superhero (super villain?). I braced myself for impact, but only felt a whoosh of air and a splatter of dirt and pine needles. Blue Cape swept by me like I didn't exist—and went straight for the dog.

"Roscoe!" he sobbed, crouching on the ground and hugging the giant poodle as if he'd been lost for months instead of a few minutes.

Roscoe responded with a wagging tail and slobbery kisses.

"Naughty, naughty puppy," Blue Cape cooed in a girly voice that seemed odd coming from a guy with stubble on his chin. "Shame on your for running away and making Frank very worried for my cutesy-doggy-sweetums."

Instead of escaping, which would have been the smart thing to do, I watched from the shadow of a cypress tree. Anyone who crooned baby-talk to a giant fur ball didn't scare me. Besides, Blue Cape (Frank) was puffing hard, like he'd run a marathon instead of a short distance downhill. If he gave me any trouble, I could easily outrun him. Cane Man (who must still be hobbling this direction) was elderly and frail enough to get knocked over by a swift breeze. Jade could have escaped from these two easily. Yet she'd waited till today.

Waited for *me*.

"Jade, you've been naughty too." Frank said disapprovingly.

I glanced around, hoping that Jade had returned and was standing behind me—but no such luck.

"What do you have to say for yourself, young lady?"

"Nothing." I pitched my voice lower to sound more like Jade.

"You shouldn't have run off. There are snakes and other dangers, so we have to stay together." Frank stood up swiftly, his expression reminding me of a teacher catching a trusted pupil cheating. "You broke the rules, but since you did it to catch Roscoe, all is forgiven. It was very sweet of you to look out for my baby puppy."

While Roscoe wasn't as gigantic as Josh's Horse, he was *far* from a puppy and reminded me of a bear with a bad perm. But I kept these thoughts to myself.

"I won't mention this to Arturo," Frank added with a conspiratorial wink—like he was doing *me* a favor.

"Um…thanks?" I said uncertainly.

"You're welcome. And thank you for catching my cutesy-fuzzy Roscoe. Bless his heart, he's still a puppy even though he's nearly twelve." He petted the dog's curly head. "Aren't you my special big guy? You just want to run and run, but you'll have to be content with our daily walk."

So that's why Frank, Cane Man, and Jade went on

walks—not for fun or health but for the dog. These people had strange priorities.

"Do you need help?" I asked as Roscoe's leash wound around Frank's ankles.

"No thanks, I don't." The dog jerked the chain so that Frank appeared to be getting down with some funky zombie dance.

"Sure you do." I covered my smile with my hand.

"Henry probably needs assistance. He took a nasty tumble."

I stared at him blankly. Henry?

"I hope he isn't bleeding. He has enough trouble keeping up on our walks." Frank gestured toward the path leading down from the dam, where Cane Man was slowly inching his way, leaning on his cane. "Jade, make sure he's okay. He wouldn't have fallen if you weren't so clumsy."

"I'm … sorry. It was an accident. I tripped on something."

"It's always something with you, isn't it?" Frank's tone sharpened, as if reminding me of previous grievances.

He turned his attention back to Roscoe, who was tugging on the leash, and tried to keep up as the dog scampered down the path. I glanced up toward the dam and Henry. He'd never catch up with me if I took off running. I could get the hell out of here now.

But I bit my lip, hesitating. The image of a bloody silver knife flashed in my head, and I knew in my gut that

I couldn't leave yet. Call it destiny, karma, or a guilty conscience, but I owed it to Josh. He was in danger and it was
my fault he was here. He never would have left everything
he cared about if I hadn't hurt him by loving Dominic
and admitting I liked being psychic. Josh couldn't change
me—so instead, he'd changed. And now he was in serious
trouble. For the sake of our friendship, for the price of
guilt, I'd stay long enough to find him.

I still didn't understand Jade's role in this place. But I
had to give her credit for wanting to help Josh. Just when I
thought I had her figured out and was comfortable hating
her, she said stuff that didn't fit.

So I'd do my best to convince Frank and Henry that I
was Jade.

"I'm sorry for knocking you down," I told the elderly
man as he hobbled toward me. "Would you like to lean
on me?"

"I can manage fine on my own, but I do appreciate the
offer, sweetheart." His voice rang out deep and resonant,
like a TV announcer. Stage presence, I thought, and guessed
he was a magician like Arturo.

When he winced, I went over to his side. "Are you in
pain?" I asked gently.

"No more than usual." He waved me off.

"Here, take my arm."

"Forget about me. Seize the opportunity, sweetheart."

"Opportunity?"

"To get the devil out of here."

"You want me to *leave?*" I asked, astonished.

"Why else would I go through this pretense? Sure, you bumped me, but I staged the fall so Frank wouldn't get wise." He stood up taller, no longer leaning on the cane. "When it comes to the art of diversion, I'm as smooth as a silk scarf."

He twirled the cane with a practiced pinch of his fingers—it was a magician's prop, not an invalid's crutch. The cane was carved with intricate stars, half-moons, and cryptic symbols, the top curved into a wolf's head with sharp carved teeth. Henry had seemed like a harmless old man, but looks could be deceiving, as I knew too well.

"You only pretended to fall, so that I could get away?"

"You bet your cute derrière I did. Danged good at it, too," he boasted. "Now get moving, sweetheart, while you can."

"Why do you want to help me?"

"Purely selfish motives." Henry smiled wryly. "Nothing personal, sweetheart, but I don't want you here. You're not one of us."

I bit my lip. Did he know I was an imposter?

"Call me old-fashioned or a chauvinist, but I don't support Arturo in this madness. Women don't belong in the brotherhood. Arty isn't thinking with the right organ," he added with a wink. "Arty and I go way back, so I understand his weaknesses and step in when he's headed for trouble."

I sensed undercurrents here, ones that Jade might understand but which only confused me. I shook my head. "I appreciate everything, but I can't go yet."

"Can't or won't?"

I thought of Josh locked up like a prisoner. "Can't," I answered.

Henry frowned. "It's your grave."

My grave or Josh's? Either way, I had a strong feeling of doom.

Henry leaned slightly on his cane. We continued down the path at a brisk pace, easily catching up with Frank, who had gotten tangled in Roscoe's leash.

The path widened and flattened. Slowing my pace, I tried to numb all my emotions, but I couldn't shake an acute sense of dread. My worries increased with each slap of my boots. How could I keep pretending to be Jade? I wouldn't know anything about the people here, except what I'd read online about Arturo and his wife. And no way could I fool Grey. I'd have to stay far away from him.

I expected Frank to make a right on the path I'd seen leading to the cabins, but instead he kept going straight, deeper into the woods until the trail turned to gravel, widened, and suddenly we were at a large sprawling house— if you could call the enormous structure a house. It was more like a gothic mansion, although its slanted roof, jutting into sharp angles like wings half-hidden in the thick pines, glinted with solar panels. A walkway paved with rocks and bordered with stone figures—all men in long cloaks—led up to the wide wooden front steps and a massive double oak door with stained-glassed windows.

Frank strode up the steps, almost tripping over energetic Roscoe before going inside.

"Wow," I said softly.

Henry patted my shoulder. "You act like you've never seen it before."

"Every time is like the first time."

"It is a beautiful resort, or hideaway, depending on your viewpoint," he added with a sly wink at me. Was this a joke Jade would understand?

When I started up the steps, Henry looked at me with puzzlement. "Where do you think you're going?"

"Um ..." I glanced down at a crack in the step.

"Did you forget your afternoon lesson?"

"How could I forget?" More like—how could I remember?

"Well, get to it before she blows a gasket. You should have escaped when you had the chance, sweetheart." He chuckled ruefully. "But since you're here, you have to stick to the schedule."

A lesson? A schedule? What sort of weirdness had Jade gotten herself involved in? And how could I find someone I didn't know in a location I'd never been to?

Playing sick might work, or faking an acute case of amnesia like I'd seen in TV soap operas. I swayed back and forth, then draped my hand across my forehead. "I'm not feeling very good ... why is everything spinning?"

Henry moved quickly for an old man, dropping his cane and putting a wrinkled arm around me. "You okay, sweetheart?"

"I—I don't know ... I'm just so dizzy. Could you take me to my lesson?"

"You can't walk ten feet? The cottage is right there."

I followed Henry's gaze over to a two-story, wood-shingled building that blended into the woods. It looked like an upside-down bowl, and its round eye-windows seemed to be watching me. I almost felt it mouthing a silent welcome from its oblong, sky-blue door.

I'd found the "cottage."

Would I find Josh inside?

After a miraculous recovery from my illness, I hurried away from Henry to knock on the cottage door. No one answered. This had to be the right place, I assured myself, so I turned the knob—and it opened easily.

High stained-glass windows sent glittery red, blue, and gold patterns down onto the tiled floor. I moved cautiously across the entryway, running my hand over the top of a marble cabinet and smelling the faint whiff of smoke coming from copper sconces trailing across the wall. My boots echoed like drum beats, slowing as I took in my surroundings. The entryway widened, and then led into a huge circular room with a vast domed ceiling. Balconies curved around two sides. From somewhere far above, lights flickered and I heard soft murmurs, like whispers.

I turned slowly in place. The bone-white walls contrasted with dark, old-fashioned furnishings: a carved bureau, a heavy oval table, a high-backed burgundy couch with an ottoman and matching loveseat, oil paintings in gilded frames, and shelves lined with thick books or odd-shaped bottles. In the center of the room, a staircase spiraled up to the balconies. Faint sounds drifted down it, so I nervously started to climb.

From the top, I peered back down for a better view, memorizing the layout of the first floor. There were two doors that led to bedrooms, along with a closed door that I guessed might be the bathroom. There was a kitchen, a dining nook, and the living room. It was almost an ordinary house—except for its shape, and the fact that its furnishings and candles belonged to another century.

"You're late."

Startled, I turned toward the sultry-sweet voice behind me and saw a face I'd seen before—in the photo of the Amazing Arturo in Josh's bedroom. But that photo was flat and lifeless; in person, the woman was incredibly vibrant, with gold-brown eyes, high cheek bones, and wide full lips. Her stunning pale-blond hair was twisted in queenlike braids around her creamy skin and, in the few steps she took toward me, her long slim legs moved as if she were dancing.

Amazing Arturo's wife and assistant: Genevieve LaFleur.

"Where have you been, Jade?" she asked, folding her arms and tapping one foot on the floor. Her attitude was pissed but I didn't care—she'd called me "Jade." Score another point for the imposter.

"I was walking and Roscoe took off. Frank was frantic," I exaggerated. "So I raced after Roscoe. He went so fast I had to push through bushes and hop rocks to catch him, but I finally grabbed his collar and brought him back. I didn't mean to be late."

Her smile was like rays of sun bursting through gray clouds. "That was sweet of you to help Frank. He dotes so terribly on that ridiculous dog. Poodles are supposed to be cute and little, not the size of a grizzly bear."

"Roscoe does look like a bear," I replied, wondering what I should call her. Mrs. Amazing Arturo didn't sound right. And LaFleur was probably her maiden name. Arturo's real last name was Pizowitz but I couldn't imagine calling this lovely, elegant woman Mrs. Pizowitz.

"We have much to do this afternoon," she said, leading me into a large room that opened off the balcony. I noticed two side doors, guessing they led to closets or another bathroom.

Jade would know exactly what she was expected to do now. All I could manage was a small nod, crossing my fingers and hoping I didn't screw up. Getting caught now would be embarrassing...and maybe even dangerous.

"Fall gracefully this time, Jade. Don't slam into the ground. I'll show you a technique that won't leave bruises and will completely fool even experienced magicians."

Slamming my body! Bruises! Again ... what was I doing here?

"Don't worry, you'll be great," she told me with an affectionate squeeze of my hand. "I don't know what I'd do without you." She clasped her hands together, rubbing a diamond wedding ring with a finger, her mouth pursed as she stared past me.

"Unlike the men around here," she added, "I know how to treat an assistant. Snapping orders and insults doesn't work, but a little kindness goes far. Remember, once everything is over tomorrow night, I'll personally drive you home."

"You will?" I couldn't figure out Jade's relationship to Genevieve. Why had she agreed to be her assistant?

"I already promised I would. I'm sorry you've had to be away from your family for so long."

"Can't I leave sooner?"

"I'd let you if it were my choice. Arty's lockdown rules are so ridiculous. No one allowed in or out until after Solstice—all to guard overrated secret rituals." Her tone was light and mocking. "Those men are such little boys, taking this all so seriously. They blame psychics for their smaller audiences today and the lack of respect for stage magicians. They're also paranoid that rogue magicians will expose their methods on TV. As if anyone would want to steal their out-dated secrets. They should be more concerned with our secrets."

She looked at me conspiratorially, as if waiting for some kind of response. But I had no idea what she was talking about, so I nodded—which seemed to be the right answer.

Genevieve turned a dimmer switch, which brightened the flickering light from the sconces. So the flames weren't real after all, only an illusion. Even the smell of candles must be artificial.

Among the fakes, I fit right in, I thought ironically.

"Well … thanks for offering to drive me home," I said, hoping to keep her talking so I could gather more information.

"I'll take you right after the ceremony. The others might object, but I'll insist," she said with a laugh. "Never underestimate the magic of a persuasive wife."

"I won't," I said, unable to be afraid of a woman who was so genuinely nice that even her aura radiated golden lights. It was impossible not to like her, and I had the feeling she'd help me if she knew about Grey's threats to Josh. I was tempted to confide in her, but she was Arturo's wife so I had to be cautious.

Genevieve walked over to a cherry-wood wardrobe and opened it to show rows of sequined, glittered, and flowing silk costumes. While her aura was light, the wardrobe oozed with a dark weight of history. When she called me over, holding out an electric blue spandex as small as a swimming suit, I found my legs going stiff with dread. I couldn't move forward, although I had no idea why.

"Here, put this on."

Everything seemed to be spinning...I could hardly stand straight. Colors and images blurred, and the walls tilted as if crashing down on me.

"Are you all right?" I heard Genevieve ask.

I held out my arms for balance, struggling to stand without falling. For a moment the dizziness calmed, and I nodded to reassure us both that everything was fine. But a heavy sense of foreboding gripped me. I shivered, staring into the wardrobe where the swirls of fabric hung like dead things.

"What's wrong, Jade? You look...different somehow. Not like yourself." She touched her finger to her chin, studying me. "Are you ill?"

Her words warbled from a far distance, although she was standing only a foot from me. Sounds, sights, smells... my five senses now faded away, leaving only one. The real world smeared colors and shapes, distorting, until only the wardrobe lurked in dark smoky hues. Fear stabbed sharply into my soul, and I sensed a presence.

Darkness swirled and mutated into a feminine shape: long copper hair, sapphire eyes, and long slim fingers that clasped a jeweled wand. A smoky hand rose up, then a whirlwind of force slammed into me, knocking me backwards.

Spinning, falling... the last thing I remembered before everything went black was the jeweled wand.

Not just an ordinary magician's wand.

Zathora's Muse.

19

"Jade!" a voice called from far away.

Hands tugged at my arms and lifted my head, and I smelled sweet lavender.

"Jade, wake up!" the voice persisted, which confused me because Jade wasn't even here. My eyes fluttered open and I stared up at Genevieve's pale, anxious face. Then it all came back to me, and I realized I was lying on the floor.

Groaning and rubbing my arm, I started to stand up,

but Genevieve bent down beside me, her skirt brushing across my leg.

"Not so fast," she cautioned. "Let me help you."

She gave me her small but surprisingly firm hand and eased me to my feet, leaning in close—too close for my comfort.

"Thank you ... I'm sorry," I said, embarrassed. "I didn't mean to ... well ... fall."

"It was a spectacular fall, although too dramatic for the fall you'll do in my act." She frowned, age lines cutting through her makeup so she looked older than I'd originally thought. "Are you all right?"

My head throbbed, but I nodded. A quick glance down showed that nothing was bleeding or broken. But the fall had shifted my wig, so my hair hung unevenly. I casually reached up to brush the bangs from my eyes, subtly adjusting the wig back into place.

"Jade, what happened?" Genevieve glanced at her wardrobe, its doors hanging open like broken wings. "You were fine one minute, then you screamed and fell."

I almost told her, but being called "Jade" reminded me to be cautious. I couldn't just blurt out that I'd seen a ghost. One major difference between Jade and myself was that I saw ghosts and she didn't. Besides, Josh's magician friends had a strong hatred for psychics and mediums. They'd never believe I saw a ghost—especially the ghost of a famous woman magician from over a century ago.

Blinking, I stared at a now-ordinary wardrobe filled with hangers draped with bright costumes. Had I really seen Zathora and her famous wand? I kept replaying the quick-flame memory, confused but not scared. Most ghosts were harmless, like Dominic's mother, who'd asked me to pass on a loving message to her son, or the ghost of a jock, who'd begged me to help the friends and family he left behind.

Ghosts existed, especially for me. But this vision had happened too fast. Already the memory of it was fading, the way you wake up from a dream and can't remember anything about it. The long hair and ethereal face were hard to visualize now. Only the wand stayed real in my mind, a spectral double of the one I'd gotten from Josh.

"Jade, please tell me what's going on." Genevieve peered around the room, shaking her head.

"I—I don't know..." My words stumbled and died on my lips. There was nothing, no hint of a ghostly aura, only rows of sequined and shimmering costumes.

"But you screamed and fell back like you were terrified. What did you see?"

"It's kind of embarrassing." I faked a blush.

"What?" She put her hands on her hips, staring at me.

"A mouse. They freak me out."

"Me too! Disgusting vermin! I hate mice." Genevieve jumped nervously, her dainty ivory and gold heels click-clacking on the hardwood floor.

I assured her the mouse was gone, eager to forget the whole weird incident. If there was a ghost hanging around, no one would know if I didn't tell them. Most ghosts were confused, lost in limbo until they found their way to the other side. If I had time before Jade sent help, I'd seek out the ghost and urge her to cross over to the light.

When Genevieve said we should begin practicing the act, I panicked because I didn't know what I was supposed to do. Even the simple act of changing into the ridiculously tiny spandex costume she gave me was a challenge—because she didn't say *where* I should change clothes. Did she expect me to strip down in front of her? It would be tricky enough squeezing into the rubber-band sized costume without messing up my wig or revealing anything about myself.

When I hesitated, Genevieve got a frustrated look on her face and gave me a push toward the closest door. So I went in, relieved to find an ordinary bathroom.

The sequins on the costume itched. I was smaller up top than Jade was, so I padded the fitted top with toilet paper.

When I stepped back into the main room, Genevieve was leaning over a long, narrow table. She placed a bronzed goblet in the center next to a plain wooden wand with no jewels, only swirls carved into the handle.

"I'm ready," I said uncertainly. "Now what should I do?"

"The usual."

Like I knew what *that* meant.

"Are you sure you don't want me to try something different?" I came up next to her, itching my arm where sequins rubbed.

"The act hasn't changed since yesterday."

"Could you show me again, so I can get it perfect?"

She frowned, irritated. "How can you forget something so simple, that you've already practiced a hundred times?"

"Only a hundred?" When in doubt, make a joke. "It was at least a million."

"Am I working you too hard? Sorry," she said, touching my cheek softly as if in apology. "But you know how important my performance is. If I don't get it right, I'll never get another chance. They don't want me here."

"They" had to be the other magicians.

"Watch carefully this time," Genevieve told me.

She stretched out her arms in a graceful welcome and smiled wide, as if facing an imaginary audience. Then she lifted the goblet to her mouth and pantomimed drinking. Suddenly her body stiffened and she gave a shrill cry. Throwing up her arms, she sank to the ground. It was quick, graceful, and so real that for a moment I almost ran to help her. But before I could move, she jumped to her feet and tilted her head at me with a now-it's-your-turn expression.

I wondered about my role in this performance and why fainting was so important. But Jade would already know this, so I didn't ask.

After practicing fainting a few times (which didn't hurt much once I mastered falling on the softer parts of my body), I learned more about Genevieve. She wasn't just Arturo's wife and assistant, but a magician, too. I encouraged her to say more, and discovered she boiled with resentment toward the "brotherhood" who didn't take her seriously. Remembering Henry's comment about women not belonging here, I didn't blame her. She'd been Arturo's assistant for decades but now wanted to perform on her own. Arturo had resisted at first, but then agreed to allow Genevieve to prove herself to the others.

Her act was based on the fairy tale of Sleeping Beauty, and she showed me her costume: flowing purple velvet with gold trimmings, a white satin lace-up bodice, and a glittering crystal crown. The costume I'd wear once we did this for real was gorgeous too: a pale green panne chiffon gown with gauzy ruffles that fell like silky petals to my ankles. I would have been nervous about performing as an assistant, except I felt sure that it was not actually going to happen. The police or Dad would show up before then ... although I was starting to wonder why it was taking Jade so long to send help.

When we finished practicing and I changed out of my costume, I hesitated before opening the wardrobe. But it was just a closet full of clothes.

Genevieve told me to rest in my room until dinner.

Problem: I didn't know where Jade's room was.

Solution: There were only two bedrooms downstairs, and when Genevieve went into one, I went into the other. And wow—what a room!

A mural of a medieval scene, complete with villagers, crude cottages, a forest with wild beasts, and a moat circling a castle spread across the walls. It was so intricate and lifelike that I felt as if I'd been transported back in time. The room's furnishings were impressive: white-gold dressers, an old brassbound trunk, beautiful woven rugs, a four-poster bed with a lacy canopy, and two glass bookshelves. I scanned the old books, recognizing many classics. I picked up a dust-jacketed copy of *Heidi's Children* that I hadn't known existed, but apparently it was the third book in a series about Heidi.

"Amy would love this," I thought. Even on modeling shoots my little sister could be found with her nose stuck into one of the vintage books from her collection. She loved the crackle of old paper and the smell of history.

Thinking about Amy made me a little sad. I missed home and felt completely shut off from my real life.

Stop feeling sorry for yourself, a snippy voice said in my head.

The book tumbled from my hands to the bed as I gave a start.

"Opal!" I cried, quickly closing my eyes and seeing

her. Over three hundred years old, she didn't look a day over thirty. "I'm so glad you're here!"

Speak with your thoughts, not audibly, Sabine, Opal cautioned, a finger to her deep-red lips. *Despite your capabilities, your naiveté renders you unable to comprehend when a situation is beyond your control.*

I smiled, confused by her words yet reassured because I wasn't completely alone anymore.

"What should I do?" I asked silently. "Everything happened so fast and I don't even know what I'm doing here."

You sought to assist a loved one, which is a true measure of your heart, and a choice I would never deter you from making.

"A loved one? You can't mean Josh!"

As usual, you jump to conclusions, allowing your emotions to confound your common sense.

"Can't you just tell me what to do minus the snarky attitude?"

Snarky? I do not recognize this uncommon term.

I chuckled. About time I confused her a little with *my* language.

But even in my mind-image, she didn't smile. Three hundred years must really kill a sense of humor. "Can you just tell me how long before help comes and I can go home?" I asked her.

I cannot impart information not within my knowledge.

"You could have just said no."

As well as you could have spoken in common terms, excluding the "snark."

"Opal, you are priceless." I longed to lift out of my body so I could hug her in astral form. Only that took too much energy and wasn't a skill I could control.

Priceless? I am not following you.

"But I'd love to follow you—right out of here," I confessed. "I can't keep pretending much longer. Josh and Grey will know I'm a fake."

Avoid the one called Grey—there is much darkness within his soul and you must not allow him close contact. But your connection to Josh goes back many lifetimes and there is much owing between your souls. Repair deep hurts by seeking him out.

"Some hurt is beyond repair." I sighed. "Josh hates me."

Hate is married to love, a window into the heart of opportunity.

"I have no idea what that means. I just know Josh won't ever speak to me again." And admitting this saddened me. Josh and I had been through a lot together. My psychic skills, buried under years of denial, had awakened that day at school when I'd saved Josh from a horrible auto shop class accident. He'd repaid me by offering his love— and I'd repaid him by betrayal. I couldn't help my feelings for Dominic, but I'd try to help Josh now.

Before I could ask Opal how to find Josh, her energy
pulled away.

I replayed everything she'd said, searching for answers
but only getting so sleepy I couldn't keep my eyes open. I
curled up against a velvet pillow on the four-poster bed. I
fell asleep and dreamed of Dominic.

He was peering down at me from the tree house, holding his hand out to help me up. But I shook my head
and gestured to my shoulders, where my backpack had
morphed into two wings. And I fluttered up to the tree
house, my wings folding into my skin and Dominic's wonderfully strong arms wrapped around me. It was like a Dis-
ney movie, with birds singing and wild animals sweeping
the floor and making lunch. A deck of cards sprang up like
an army and marched up to the table, shuffled themselves,
then flipped into neat piles. Dominic and I played for
hours, and he won so often that I joked he must be cheating and as a penalty, he owed me a kiss...

He leaned toward me, grasping my hands and pulling
me against his warm chest. I could smell a fresh outdoor
odor and hear his heart speeding up. I lifted my chin and
tasted his sweet breath as he parted his lips...

But before his lips could touch mine, a monstrous
bird swooped through the window and clawed my hair
and flew away. "Dominic, Dominic!" I screamed.

Then my eyes snapped open. I looked around, disappointed not to see tree tops. If only I could slip back into
the dream...with Dominic.

"So who is this Dominic?" Genevieve stood over me, clearly amused.

"Um ... just a friend. How long have I been sleeping?"

"Three hours. You must have really been tired. Come on, it's time for dinner."

It had been forever since breakfast, a quick cream-cheese bagel before I started my drive up to the mountains. I should be starving, but my stomach was too knotted with anxiety.

I followed Genevieve outside and down the path toward the mansion. Walking past the forbidding statues of long-dead magicians and up the steps, I paid close attention to my surroundings so I could find my way out if I needed a quick escape.

My heart quickened when we entered a huge, narrow room lined with long wooden tables. Men in capes and robes crowded together, talking and laughing. Platters were passed from hand to hand and the magicians reached out, helping themselves to bread and steaming meat. Flagons of wine were filled and refilled. I felt like I'd stepped onto a movie set.

I was both guest and captive here. The men mostly ignored me. I scanned faces, seeking the one I'd once loved. I didn't see Josh, but it was easy to spot Arturo right away, front and center, his face rapt with attention as he spoke to a slender, dark-skinned man with hoops in his ears. The Amazing Arturo oozed charisma. Gazes were fixed on him, and everyone near him was captivated by whatever he was saying. No one glanced up as Genevieve led me to a small round table by the kitchen.

"Why aren't you sitting with Arturo?" I asked, glancing up as a waiter in a brown apron set heaping bowls on our table.

"I wondered when you'd ask." Genevieve grimaced in the direction of her husband. "As merely the assistant to the Amazing Arturo, I used to be relegated to eating in the kitchen. So this table is quite an upgrade."

"But you're his wife."

"That means nothing here. Wives are not allowed, so it's fortunate I'm also Arturo's assistant. It's an honor for us to be in the presence of all these great chauvinistic men ... or so I've been told many times."

The bitterness in her words was sharper than the knife she pulled from a pocket to slice her buttery roll in half. Her eyes narrowed as she plopped the roll into her mouth.

Oh, touchy subject. Not going there again. I looked around the room once more, up and down each table, searching for Josh.

He wasn't here—but I saw Grey with others wearing similar dark cloaks. But no one else had a long white-blond ponytail. Grey caught me looking, narrowed his dark eyes at me, and returned to eating.

I did *not* make the mistake of looking at him again.

Genevieve's bitter mood passed and we chatted about

light, meaningless topics as we ate. This was a stark change from the dedicated magician I'd practiced with a short while ago. It was like she was masquerading, too—as Arturo's flighty wife rather than a magician equal to or perhaps better than the others in this room.

All the while, I was thinking hard, trying to figure out how to search for Josh. Grey would know—but I didn't have the nerve to ask him. Maybe I could follow him to see if he'd lead me to Josh. If I got the chance, I'd try it. But even if I had complete freedom to go wherever I wanted (which I doubted), this building was huge and it would be easy to get lost. I'd passed about twelve hallways and three staircases just on the short walk to the dining hall. I wished Thorn were here with her Finding skill.

Noisy pot banging, conversation, and busy activity from the kitchen caught my attention. The shuttered doors flung open with a gush of heated, savory air and two elderly waiters, one stout with slicked-back white hair and the other beanpole-skinny with a scraggly beard, delivered food trays to the tables. Both looked weary, their dingy-brown aprons flapping like feeble birds as they hurried to keep up with the demanding diners.

Then a different waiter came out of the kitchen doors, his head down in concentration as he balanced a large tray with covered dishes. Instead of heading for the tables, he went the opposite direction and slipped out the front door.

I didn't have Thorn's gift for Finding, but sometimes I just knew things. And I knew in the depth of my soul that if I followed that waiter, I'd find Josh.

Impulsively, I jumped up from the table, "accidentally" dumping my plate all over myself. Buttered bread, a cob of corn, and a barbecued drumstick spilled down my jeans to the floor. "Sorry!" I cried, as bloodlike sauce dripped down my legs. "I'll go clean up and change my clothes."

Genevieve looked like she was going to protest, but I didn't give her a chance.

I ran from the room—to rescue the boy I used to love.

20

I caught up with the waiter as he made a sharp left down a high-ceilinged hallway. I pressed against a wall. I felt sticky wetness sliding into my shoes and plucked a kernel of corn off my pockets.

Then I was moving again, as the waiter turned another corner. This hall was narrower and ended at a staircase leading down. I hung back, careful not to be seen. As one of the few women in this place, I didn't exactly blend in.

I listened to the waiter's footsteps clanging softly on

the stairs and once he was far enough ahead, I moved cautiously down the staircase. Ducking low, I saw the waiter slow down and then stop in front of a door near the end of the hall. He set the plate down, then reached up to knock on the door. I waited for the door to open.

Only it never did.

Instead, there was a low murmur of conversation as a narrow wooden panel in the door flipped open. The tray of food was grasped by a flash of hands, then disappeared into the room and the panel banged shut. Anger seethed through me. Poor Josh! How much suffering was he enduring in this prison?

The waiter turned to leave—heading back my direction.

Frantically, I looked around for somewhere to hide. I'd never make it back up the stairs without being seen. Then I noticed a small shadowy hole beneath the stairs and flung myself inside—just as his footsteps hurried past.

Once all sounds had faded except for the roaring of my own mind, I stood up and walked down the hall. I passed two doors, then stopped in front of the door that the waiter had delivered the food to. I closed my eyes and sought out the energy inside—and I knew I'd found him.

But when I lifted my hand to knock, I hesitated. What was I going to say to Josh? The last time we'd spoken, he'd called my psychic ability a tool of the devil. His mind was closed to anything that wasn't clearly explained with science. In his opinion, magic was merely a form of entertainment using logical illusions. Ghosts didn't exist. When people died, that was the last you heard from them.

And nothing I could say to Josh would ever change his mind.

So I wouldn't even try. I'd come here as his friend, and as his friend, I'd warn him about Grey and convince him to come away with me.

Mustering courage, I knocked once, then twice, on the door.

"Did you forget something?"

Josh's voice. It was startling, although it was what I'd expected. I hardly knew what to say and stood there, unsure what to do next.

"What do you want now?" Josh called through the closed door.

I stared, startled when an arm reached out through the door flap, palm up in questioning.

Memory swept me back to warm nights in Josh's arms, tasting his gentle kisses and listening to his stories of entertaining sick kids with magic tricks. For a few weeks, I'd thought I loved him. Maybe I had, or maybe I'd just been crushing because he was so smart, kind, and likeable. But "like" wasn't enough.

"Hey Josh," I said softly.

"What the—! SABINE!" he choked out, jerking his arm back inside.

"Yeah, it's me."

"No, you can't be here."

"Really, it's me."

"I—I can hardly think! I mean, what are you doing here?"

"Horse missed you."

"You came here to tell me Horse missed me?" He groaned, then laughed—a brittle sound that swept me with a wave of sadness, bringing back our dog-walk dates with Horse, holding hands and just enjoying being together.

"So, can you to let me in?" I asked, leaning one hand on the door.

"No. The door is locked."

I jiggled the knob but it didn't open.

"What's going on, Josh? Jade told me you were locked in, but it seemed so unbelievable."

"Did Jade send you?" His tone sharpened. "Grey never should have let her come here. Did he bring you here too?"

"No, I came on my own."

"Why?"

"To find you."

"You did that for me?" he asked softly.

"And for Horse," I added, before he got the wrong idea.

Josh laughed. "How is he?"

"Not so hot since you left, but Dominic told me he was doing much better."

"Dominic?" Josh dropped the name as if it were a bomb. "What was he doing with *my* dog?"

"Encouraging him to eat and get over missing you," I said accusingly. "Dominic doesn't let personal feelings stop him from helping an animal."

"Of course not—he's a saint." I winced at Josh's biting sarcasm. "So how's it working out with you two?"

"Just great. Except he's not..." I couldn't finish.

"Except what?"

"He's away, that's all. He's dealing with some... um ... family issues."

"No guy would stay away from you too long."

"Thanks, Josh. That's really sweet."

"Like being sweet is a good thing," he scoffed. "Girls go for the tough, mysterious guys."

"Someday you'll find the right girl."

"I thought I already had," he said sadly. "But the best lessons are learned from mistakes—at least that's what Arturo tells me whenever I screw up a trick. How did you get in here without him knowing, anyway? There are cameras, electric fencing, and guards patrolling the property. We're in lockdown—no one goes in or out."

"I squeezed under a break in the fence and climbed down from the dam."

"And no one stopped you?"

"Well... not exactly." I glanced around nervously. How long before another waiter or someone else came along? "Josh, I came here because I was worried about you. You may not realize it, but you're in terrible danger."

"Danger?" he said skeptically. "Don't be ridiculous."

"You can't trust Grey. He told Jade he'd kill you if she left here."

"That's bull. Grey's my bro. He'd never betray me." *Not like you did*, his tone implied.

"Jade said he forced her to help him with cruel magic tricks—and I saw knife cuts on her arm. He tortured her, Josh! Don't trust him! Come away with me."

"Does this have anything to do with your psychic crap?" His tone had cooled, no longer friendly. "Was my danger something you read in tarot cards or heard in a séance?"

"No," I lied, flashing back to my vision of Josh stabbing himself with a knife.

"Well, I still don't get how you got past the security," he muttered.

I touched a curl of fake red hair. "Look through the door flap."

The rectangular flap flipped up, and I had a glimpse of Josh's dark eyes through the narrow opening. "Jade!" I heard him gasp. Then the flap banged shut.

"Everyone thinks I'm Jade," I admitted. "That's how I can stay here. I'm worried about you."

"I'm nothing to you anymore. Don't waste your worry on me."

"It's not wasted. No matter what you think, I still care what happens to you. Maybe not the way ... well, the way it was ... but as a friend. When your mom said you were gone, I was afraid you were in trouble and wanted to help. That's why I'm here."

"Sabine ... I don't know what to say."

"Say you'll leave this place with me."

"It's not that simple," he said, his tone softening.

"Is there any other way out of your room?"

"No. But Sabine, you've got it all wrong. I'm not a prisoner."

"Then why else would you be locked in?"

"For secrecy. It's a tradition for initiates to work in isolation. The door may be locked, but I'm the one with the key. I can leave any time if I want."

"Then why do you stay here?" I asked.

"To practice my act for my initiation."

"At the Solstice ceremony," I said, frowning.

"Yes. Tomorrow night I'll finally become a full member of Arturo's brotherhood of magicians. Normally I wouldn't be invited to audition until I turned eighteen, but Arturo knew I was unhappy and needed to get away from, well ... you know."

Oh, I knew. He needed to get away from me.

"Only one apprentice is allowed to join the society a year," Josh added. "Most years no one auditions, but this year there are two of us hoping to be chosen. To win, I need to astonish everyone with my performance, so I'm working in total secrecy."

I'd known that being a professional magician meant a lot to Josh, but hearing the pride and excitement in his voice made me realize just *how* important.

"So you won't leave with me?" I asked.

"No. But I promised Mom I'd be home for Christmas, so I'll only be here a few more days. By then I should be a professional magician."

"Does this have something to do with the PFC tattoo on your arm?"

"No, that was all Grey's idea. Arturo has one, so Grey and I had it done too. It's supposed to be secret, but you should know—since it explains why I was so freaked to see you at a séance. It's our personal vow to uphold the science of magic."

I winced. "So what does it mean?"

"Performers against Frauds and Charlatans."

I could hardly believe what I was hearing. His tone held anger and judgment. I tried to understand where he was coming from, although I knew he'd been influenced by his mentor for years. When the Amazing Arturo said psychics were all fakes, Josh believed it with his whole heart.

"Some psychics might be frauds," I told him, "but some are real."

"I'm sorry you believe that." His words shut me out as divisively as the heavy wood door I was leaning against.

"And I'm sorry you don't." I sighed. "I'm sorry for ... well, everything."

There was a silence full of the things neither one of us could say. Then the door flap jiggled and Josh reached out again. I hesitated, then entwined my fingers with his. It was part apology, but mostly good-bye.

Then our fingers slipped apart ... and the door flap closed.

"I—I better go," I said awkwardly.

"Yeah ... you should. But thanks ... this has meant a lot to me."

I wasn't sure what he meant, but asking would only make things harder.

I started to leave, but thought of something and turned back.

"Just one more thing."

"What?"

"Who's the apprentice you'll be competing against?"

"I thought you already knew." Josh paused. "It's Grey."

*   *   *

Dread weighed me down, making it hard for me to breathe as I made my way back down the hall and up the stairs. Grey was Josh's competition—and Grey had threatened to kill him. But Josh wouldn't believe this any more than he believed that the ghost of his older brother would pop in for a visit.

If only I could manage a small miracle like that— arrange a reunion with Josh and the brother he'd lost too soon. But ghosts chose to come to me, not the other way around.

There wasn't anything else I could do here. I'd found Josh, and he was fine. For now. He wouldn't leave before his initiation performance. It was tempting to stick around to watch the show, but I didn't belong here. My family and friends must be worried about me and I couldn't wait to get home.

But I'd have to wait till morning. I'd never find the trail back in the dark unless I could find a flashlight. Did anyone even have a flashlight around here? They all seemed so back-in-time, I'd have a better chance of finding a torch. But it wouldn't hurt to search for a flashlight, since there was nothing keeping me here now. Genevieve could find another assistant. I wouldn't be around for the show.

Lost in my thoughts, I wasn't paying attention as I stepped out of the main house and started down the front steps. I'd only taken a few steps when I heard the sound. A thud, like a footstep. Before I could turn, a hand reached out. Sharp fingernails stabbed into my wrist, and I felt hot breath near my ear.

"Where do you think you're going ... *Sabine?*"

21

"Let go," I cried, trying to shake off Grey's grip.

"Answer my question," Grey demanded, his fingernails digging into my skin. "Where were you going?"

"To Genevieve's cottage, not that it's any of your business." I glared at the freakishly white-blond hair on his young, sharp-angled face. Half-hidden under a hooded cloak, Grey looked more ghostlike than a real ghost.

"Where's the real Jade?"

"You think I have a clone?" I bluffed. "There's only

one Jade, and you're really pissing her off right now. Let go of me."

"I know who you are—and you're definitely not Jade. Maybe you can fool the others around here, but I've met both of you. Where is she?"

"I don't know." It was the truth. I had no sense of where she was now, although I hoped and prayed she'd told someone where I was and that help was on the way.

"You're lying—but then that's what you do best. You do not want to cross me. So I'll ask again, nicely." He smiled in a sicko way that made me think of serial killers in horror movies. "Where is Jade?"

"You're hurting me. If you don't let go, I'm going to scream very loud."

"Scream and I really will hurt you." He leaned close to my face and I expected his breath to smell wicked, like sulfur, but it was sweet like the buttery bread from dinner.

"Just leave me alone," I snapped.

"You want to be treated like Jade?" he asked in a low, mocking tone. We were standing so close together that anyone glancing in our direction might think we were good friends. But Grey's aura was darkened with hate and cruelty. Furious energy pulsed from him as he fanned his long cloak out, revealing a row of glinting daggers tucked into pockets of the dark fabric.

In a quicksilver move, he whipped out a unicorn-hilted dagger and pressed the cold blade against my throat.

I froze, as still as the solemn statues that lined the walkway. "Don't," I whimpered.

"Then do exactly what I say."

"W—what?"

"For tonight, be my lovely assistant and create the illusion that you are mine," he said with a dry chuckle. "It's what they expect anyway, since when Jade came here I let them assume she was my girl."

"She's not, and I won't pretend to be," I hissed.

The knife slipped slightly, pricking my skin. Tears swam in my eyes.

"Walk now—back up the steps and into the lower-east wing. My room isn't far from Josh's room, which I know you just visited. Initiate rooms are private—not even Master Arturo will come in unless I invite him. But I've only invited one person. Can you guess who?"

He didn't lower the knife, so I didn't dare answer.

"Jade," he told me. "Of course, you know—you've been conspiring with her all along. Is that why you're masquerading in her place? I could force you to tell me where she is, but it doesn't matter. One girl is as good as another. That's why your secret is safe with me."

"You aren't going to tell anyone who I really am?" I asked, surprised.

"Why cause unnecessary complications? Jade is too afraid of me to tell anyone—she knows what I'll do to Josh if she blabs. Besides, it'll be over tomorrow night."

Solstice, I thought. Everything seems to come back to the initiation ceremony. But Grey was wrong about Jade. She would bring help back. She was my sister and I trusted her.

"I'm going to make magician history once I win the competition," he told me.

"What if Josh wins instead of you?"

"I've made sure I'll win," he said with a cunning smile. "My stage name will be known worldwide: 'The Grey Ghost.' My act will prove that ghosts are only illusion, and denounce fakers and charlatans like you and your grandmother and that candy-store bitch."

He meant Velvet, and I shuddered. His aura smothered me like molten ash, making me weak and confusing my thoughts. No wonder Jade had been so scared of him.

"Watch your step—I wouldn't want you to slip," Grey said with a wry chuckle, his grip still iron-clad. "Your heart pounds so fast. Afraid of me?"

I pursed my lips defiantly.

We went down the same stairs that had led me to Josh earlier. I could see Josh's room five doors down. I longed to call out to him, but I couldn't with a knife at my throat. If only Josh would open his door and look out, he'd see the truth about Grey. But we stopped suddenly at a heavy door with no windows.

Grey slipped the knife back underneath his cape but kept a firm grip on my arm as he withdrew a set of keys from a pocket.

"Smile like we're just out for a walk," he warned. "My magic act is all about the brutal swiftness of the knife. If you try to run, I'll drop you with a knife before you make it to the stairs. Then I'll go after Josh."

"He's your friend."

"He's my competition."

"Jade told me you threatened to kill him."

"I'll do what's necessary," he said, as if bragging. "Words hold great power, but actions speak louder. I warned Jade what would happen if she left."

"Leave Josh alone!"

"It's not as if he'd be much of a loss. Josh only plays at being a magician."

"You're afraid he'll beat you in the competition," I accused him.

"Not even," he scoffed.

I mentally called out to Opal and any other spirits close by, a scream heard only inside my head. But there was no answer. I glanced down the hall again, sending out a silent SOS to Josh. *Open the door. Look down the hall. Please— before Grey forces me into his room and...* well, I didn't know and was terrified to find out.

"Aren't you curious about my act?" Grey said, his tone light, as if he enjoyed toying with me like a cat bats around a mouse before going in for the kill. "All the brotherhood will be astonished when they see the illusions I've created. It's nearly ready, but a dress rehearsal could be interesting with you to assist me."

He paused, studying me, then continued.

"When I reveal my act to the brotherhood, I'll invite one of them to assist me. But they can't practice with me or they'd learn my secrets. You'll get a sneak-peak of the performance tonight—just like when Jade worked with me, before Master Arturo asked her to assist his wife."

"I saw the cuts on her arm," I told him.

"Unfortunately, Jade was clumsy. But I know you'll try harder."

He lifted his hand, a key poised to open his door. *Stall him!* a voice shouted in my head. *Do not go in that room!*

"What will I have to do?" I asked. "I don't know anything about stage tricks."

"Not tricks—the art of illusion."

"What's the difference?"

He gave me an are-you-really-that-stupid look.

"My stage branding will be blades." He stared off as if seeing his name in lights on a marquee. "You've heard of a magician cutting his assistant in half?"

"Isn't that kind of cliché?"

"Not my version. I slice my assistant into fractions. Hair slithers from a head like escaping snakes, eyes fall from sockets and float in the air, and blood pools into a whirlwind that sweeps out to my audience. And you, Fake-Jade, will assist me tonight in a pract—"

"Jade!" a woman's voice interrupted.

Grey and I both whirled toward the staircase where

Genevieve stood. Her hands were on her hips and her face was flushed with irritation.

"I've been looking everywhere for you!" Genevieve complained. "Why didn't you come back to dinner? I told you we weren't finished working today."

"You did?" My throat was so dry with fear my voice came out raspy.

"Don't pretend you don't remember. You can't hide out with your boyfriend to avoid work. I'm sorry to steal her away, Grey, but I need her assistance."

Grey's hands dropped, too casually, to his sides.

"Of course," he said, with a dismissive gesture toward me. "She's all yours."

"Come on, Jade. You've really disappointed me."

"I'm sorry," I told her.

But I wasn't at all sorry. I was relieved and grateful. Although Genevieve was acting annoyed, I knew she was pretending. Her aura was pulsing with bright shades of shrewd awareness. She had a good idea what was going on.

She was here to rescue me.

With a glance down at the burning red marks on my arm, I eagerly—gratefully—accepted the rescue.

*   *   *

Genevieve didn't speak on the short walk back to her cottage. I wondered what she was thinking and how much she knew. But she didn't ask any questions, so neither did I.

When we reached the cottage, she didn't lead me upstairs for more practice. She offered me a glass of milk and a crispy apple tart.

"The dessert you missed," she said kindly.

Cooked apples never tasted so good.

A short while later, as I slipped on an old-fashioned cotton nightgown, I told myself I would leave in the morning. Jade hadn't sent help, so I was on my own.

I slept soundly—I saw no ghosts and didn't astral-travel or get any messages from Opal. While the rest felt good, I was disappointed that the other side had abandoned me as well. To make things worse, the sky the next morning was dark with heavy clouds, threatening rain.

Slipping back into yesterday's clothes, I readjusted my wig and applied some makeup I found on a mirrored dresser. I resumed my role as Jade.

The cottage was silent except for the whistling of wind that shivered the windows. I wandered around, not sure what I should do. Was breakfast served in the dining room? Should I go on my own, or wait for Genevieve?

Her bedroom door was ajar, so I peeked inside. She wasn't there. I was starting up the stairs when I heard a sound and saw her coming in the front door, carrying a basket full of blossoming flowers.

"Good morning, Jade." She greeted me so warmly that I felt a little guilty for planning to leave. I hoped she could find someone else to be her assistant.

"What are those for?" I pointed to the basket.

"Enjoyment. Fresh flowers are beautiful and smell wonderful. Wait a minute while I put them in a vase then we'll go to breakfast. Are you hungry?"

I nodded.

The dining room wasn't very full, only a few men at the main table. I waved to Frank, who was busy in the kitchen, then enjoyed fruit, sausage, and fluffy biscuits. Genevieve told me about her travels with her husband and how she was always so proud to work alongside him. They'd performed all around the world, which seemed very romantic. Her stories were interesting and showed me her softer side.

"Poor Arty doesn't understand why I want to be a magician, too, not merely his assistant. He's cross with me," she admitted sadly. "But he's giving me a chance. He's taken a lot of flack for it, too, from the brotherhood. It'll be tough to win their respect. But I'm determined to succeed."

"You will," I said, knowing my words would come true. But I also had a sense of a warning, as if her dreams would come at a high cost.

I hoped to sneak away after breakfast, but Genevieve wanted to practice the act again. It seemed kind of simple. All I had to do was drink some water from a cup, then pretend to faint. I didn't understand how this could amaze anyone, but then, I wasn't a magician.

As I practiced with Genevieve, I could sense a presence hovering close by. Zathora's ghost, I thought, eyeing the wardrobe. Her death had been so tragic and things hadn't improved much if she was still hanging around. I could guide her to the other side, if I could speak to her alone.

When Genevieve announced that we were done and said she was going to take a nap, I felt a ripple of excitement. I could finally leave! But why not take a few minutes before I left to help Zathora cross over?

I went to my room and waited about twenty minutes. Then I tiptoed to the staircase, glancing over at Genevieve's closed bedroom door. I stepped softly on the stairs, careful to avoid the middle one that sometimes creaked. At the top of the stairs, I hesitated, trying to remember what Nona had told me about helping ghosts stuck in limbo. *Be confident, and tell them firmly it's time to go to the light.*

As I reached out to open the door, I stopped.

Was I hearing voices from inside?

Pressing my ear against the wood, I listened. Yes, definitely voices, both female. Genevieve and another voice I didn't recognize, which spoke with a rolling accent, perhaps Spanish or Italian.

"…all ready for tonight." Genevieve's voice rose with excitement. "I can hardly believe it's going to finally happen. All the planning and preparation leading to this amazing night."

"You'll be the amazing one in the family from here on," the other woman said warmly. She sounded younger than Genevieve.

"I've wanted to have my own act for years. I'm tired of being ignored, considered merely the magician's wife. Even when I assist him, I'm only another stage prop. But thanks to you, all that will change," Genevieve said. "I never would have had the courage, much less the skill. You've taught me so much."

"I shall rejoice in your success," the other woman said. "Did you find the herbs I described?"

"Yes—exactly where you told me."

"And the girl?"

"She's eager to do what I ask." Genevieve laughed. "I made sure of her loyalty by having Grey lean on her. I'm not comfortable with Grey's methods, but since he wants my influence with Arturo to ensure that he wins the competition, he's been very helpful. Jade was so relieved when I showed up and whisked her away."

I covered my mouth so I wouldn't gasp. Grey working with Genevieve? I could hardly believe it, and leaned against the door, straining to hear more.

"Clever Genevieve," the other woman praised her. "The art of persuasion is a subtle form of illusion."

"Jade is so grateful, and she trusts me completely."

"But can we trust her? She seems different... almost like she is a different person. I am puzzled and wrought with unease. I think she sighted me yesterday."

"Impossible! No one knows about you except me."

"I certainly hope you're right. Much is at stake tonight. Nothing must go wrong."

"It won't. You've taught me so much, and I am confident all will go smoothly. I've already crushed the herbs, so all that's left is to slip them into her drink."

"Mix it right before you give it to her. Are you positive she'll drink it?"

"I told her it would be fruit punch. She doesn't suspect a thing."

"Excellent," the other woman said approvingly. "Now all that's left is the finale, where you'll ..."

Her words were fading along with her footsteps as she moved farther away from the door. I think Genevieve replied, but I could only hear a faint murmur of her voice. I had to know more. So I carefully grasped the knob and twisted, slowly, until there was a soft click. The door inched open.

Leaning forward, I peered through the crack. Genevieve's back was to me as she bent over the table I'd sat on during practice, her hand clasped around the goblet I'd drunk from. When we rehearsed, it had been filled with water—but what would I be drinking during the performance?

Not fruit punch ...

I leaned in closer and my gaze swept the room for the other woman. At first I didn't see her, but suddenly there she was, beside Genevieve—her shining copper hair and almost glowing skin a starling contrast to Genevieve's fair skin and coiffed blond hair.

"The words I've taught you and the jewels will burn with powerful energy," the copper-haired woman was saying. "Once she's dead, we'll make magician history."

I covered my mouth, stunned, staring at this woman.

I could see right through her.

Zathora.

22

It didn't take a math degree to add up who was supposed to die on stage.

Well, count me out of here.

I backed up and practically ran down the stairs. I didn't have a plan but I couldn't stay here one more minute—not when the woman I thought was a friend wanted to kill me, and her accomplice was already dead.

How could I have been so wrong about Genevieve? If I didn't have the ability to see and hear ghosts, I wouldn't have found out a thing. Genevieve had totally conned me—even her aura hadn't given her away. But at least I found out in time. And, if I hadn't taken Jade's place, Jade would have been in danger without even knowing it. She would have been led to the stage altar like a sacrifice victim.

But I had learned the truth in time to get away. I sent a grateful thanks to Opal, Nona, Velvet, and all my psychic mentors.

I stepped outside and the chilly wind slammed into me. The weather had changed; dense white-gray clouds churned with stormy fury. I inhaled the acrid warning of rain and clutched my shivering arms. Please let me escape before the sky opens up and attacks, I thought.

The wind whipped harder and I wished I had my jacket, but there was no turning back.

"Once she's dead, we'll make magician history." The memory of these words taunted me, urging my feet to move faster.

But why was Genevieve plotting to kill me? How could she expect to get away with it? The brotherhood may guard their secrets, but I doubted they'd approve of murder. Watching someone die was *not* a magic trick.

Or maybe I'd misunderstood what I'd heard, and my "dying" was simply part of the act. I had practiced how to faint so it looked like I had fallen into a deep sleep. But sleep wasn't the same as dead. When Zathora gave her infamous final performance, she hadn't planned to die on stage; she'd expected to create a miracle of bringing herself back to life. Was that Genevieve's plan? To create the illusion of killing me, then bringing me back to life? How would Genevieve prove I was dead? Parade my lifeless body for the audience to examine? Not if I had anything to say about it!

But what ticked me off even more was all the fainting practice Genevieve made me do when she knew I wouldn't need to fake it. If I drank the poison, my fall would be the real thing.

So not going to happen.

Genevieve could cancel the show or drink the damned poison herself.

Wind buffeted against me as I hurried farther away from the cottage, too angry to feel its sharp chilly bite. I turned onto the path that had brought me here yesterday. Pine needles crunched beneath my feet as the gravel path turned to rough dirt, and some of the anxiety in my heart eased when I saw the gleaming white dam in the distance.

Freedom was so close...

I heard the bark and something slammed into me. Knocked down, I couldn't breathe. Something large pressed on top of me. Gasping, I looked up just as a slobbery doggy tongue licked my face.

"Oooh! Get off!" I groaned.

"Sorry, but Roscoe gets so excited when it's time to take our walk." Frank stood over me, his wrinkles crinkling in a smile. He bent down with his hand out and I thought he would offer me a hand up, but instead he just pulled on Roscoe's collar.

"Keep him away from me."

"He just doesn't know his strength. Don't be mad. Come on, let's walk."

"Walk?" I pushed myself off the ground, my palms stinging with red gravel marks. "Are you serious? Just look at the sky, it's going to rain soon."

"Roscoe needs his walk."

"And a little rain never killed anyone," a sardonic voice cut in.

He'd moved so silently, I hadn't heard him come up beside us. But now I could feel his predatory aura. "What are you doing here?"

Grey shrugged, his pale brows arched as if amused. "Taking a walk. Henry isn't feeling well so I'm going with you."

"Glad to have you," Frank said cheerfully. "The more the merrier. Right?"

I refused to reply "right," since everything about Grey was wrong.

"It'll be fun ... Jade," Grey said, with a mocking grin just for me. Then he stroked his cloak, running his fingers over the place where his knives were hidden under the fabric. A subtle but very effective threat.

I started walking.

*　　*　　*

Grey stayed uncomfortably close, his keen gaze keeping track of me at all times. I even tried Jade's trick of bumping into Frank so that Roscoe broke loose. I sprinted off as if I planned to chase the dog, then turned in the opposite direction, toward the path I knew would take me back to the road. I'd made it only a few yards before a silver missile buzzed passed my head. A knife lodged itself into a patch of yellow wildflowers, narrowly missing me.

"Sorry," Grey said as he came over to grab his knife.

"Yeah, sorry you missed."

"I never miss." He rubbed the knife on his cloak. "Were you going somewhere?"

He knew I had tried to escape and I knew that he knew. Why bother to pretend? I turned my back to him and hurried to catch up with Frank and Roscoe.

As I followed the graveled path, I felt Grey's eyes boring into me. Watching to make sure I didn't try to escape.

It started to pour just as we reached the main house, and I was drenched in the short distance to the cottage. Despite the rain, I didn't lose all hope for escape. Once Grey left me, I'd sneak out again.

But Grey didn't leave me; he led me inside the cottage and stayed. He took Genevieve aside and whispered in her ear. I didn't need to be psychic to know that he was warning her not to let me out of her sight. And while Grey went off to his private work room, Genevieve stared at me in a new, suspicious way. Then suddenly she had chores for me to do.

When I finished alphabetizing her bottled spices, she gave me a large wooden box full of crystals, from pinky-small to palm-sized and glittering in shades of mauve, yellow, lavender, and translucent. She kept checking on me, warning me not to drop the precious stones. I was careful, but I was also watching her from the corner of my eye as she filled a box with candles, matches, rolls of fabric, and the goblet.

When she announced she was leaving to set up for the performance, my blood chilled. Time was running out—and so was daylight. I tapped my fingers on the table, watching Genevieve, mentally urging her to leave so I could do the same.

But as she walked out the door, Frank strode in, leading Roscoe. He made up some lame story about needing help grooming Roscoe. But the look he exchanged with Genevieve on her way out told the real story. He was there to guard me.

Sure, I could outrun him. But when he casually mentioned that Grey was close by "if we needed any help with Roscoe," my escape plans died.

So I followed Frank and his curly dog upstairs to the workroom. Grooming Roscoe wasn't hard work, but it was messy. Fuzzy dog hair kept flying in my face and even up my nose.

Holding the leash with one hand and batting away flying fur with the other, my mind wandered … not very far,
just downstairs to the front door that led to freedom. I had
to get out of here before dark! If I didn't escape soon, I
wouldn't get another chance. But with Grey close by, how
could I sneak away? I couldn't run faster than he could
throw a knife. And there was Josh to consider too. It would
be really easy for Grey to eliminate his competition with a
knife "accident."

Roscoe squirmed, nearly slipping from my grasp. But
I was quick and held him tight.

"Thanks, Jade," Frank said, smiling at me. But beneath
his smile, was he a friend or foe? I suspected he had a strong
loyalty to Grey and the brotherhood.

I wished for someone loyal to me … like Dominic. If
he knew I was in trouble, he'd come after me. He'd send
his animal posse out searching until they found me and I
was safe back at home. But he was in worse trouble, probably locked in a jail cell, sinking into depression. I couldn't
feel his energy—it was as if he was beyond reach far, far
away. I ached with loneliness.

The only friend I had here was Josh. But even if I did
ask him for help, he'd never believe that I'd overheard Genevieve plotting with a ghost. And no one knew where I
was—except Jade. Already a day had passed and she hadn't
kept her promise. Perhaps she never meant to.

And it hurt to know that Genevieve was willing to

sacrifice me for a magic trick. Even worse, she'd conspired with Grey in a form of bad cop/good cop. The betrayal hurt more than it should, given that I'd only known Genevieve a day. I decided that when she asked me to change into my costume tonight, I would refuse. No more would I be her willing victim.

I would *not* go on stage and drink poison.

Frank snapped me out of my thoughts. "Jade, could you bring Roscoe a bowl of water?"

Nodding, I walked to the sink. I was moving on autopilot now, an almost peaceful numbness settling over me.

As water spilled into the sink, my gaze swept over to the cabinet where I'd organized bottles of spices earlier. When I cleaned things up, I'd noticed the flowers she'd gathered in the morning discarded in the garbage. Or, I'd thought they were flowers, but now I realized that their purpose was much more deadly—and from the golden-green fragments left behind, I was sure she'd already crushed the potion.

Staring into running water, visions and sounds sailed me back into time ...

In the dank depths of an old building, a whisper carried beyond life and death—and was heard. A shadow slithered from smoke, reaching, stretching, until a distinct shape emerged. Slender arms and legs, dark sapphire eyes, copper hair dancing with the flames, and a dazzling jeweled wand in her hand.

"Who calls Zathora forth?" the shadow woman demanded.

"I do." A red-robed figure pulled back her hood. Gen-evieve. "I have read your diaries and letters. You stunned and confounded the chauvinistic world of magicians with your most astonishing last performance."

"Do you mock me?" Her eyes blazed with bitterness. "My legacy was failure; the living are unaware of my great achievements."

"But I know your greatness," Genevieve said in excited fervor. "You succeeded where all other magicians failed—you discovered how to bring the dead back to life. Reveal the secret to me and I'll make you more famous in death than life. Magicians will honor you."

"Honor won't suffice," the shadow woman hissed. "But I shall reveal what you request, not for fame but for vengeance. Be warned, though, for secrets are not given freely—the cost of life is death. On Solstice night, bring forth a comely young maiden with no knowledge of her sacrifice."

"A sacrifice?" There was hesitation, then Genevieve nod-ded. "Agreed."

"Our bargain is sealed. My secrets will be yours—when the girl dies."

The scene shifted, rushing forward in time.

I saw myself on stage, my fake red hair tumbling against my glossy gown. Red candles glowed in a circle around a raised altar, not the hard metal table I'd used for practice. And glit-tering crystals were strung on a canopy above the altar, spar-kling with tinkling song. I moved forward slowly, as if in a *trance, on an ornamental rug designed with stars and half-moon symbols that were similar to what I'd seen on Henry's cane.*

Cloaked magicians watched with silent skepticism. Beside me on stage, Genevieve glowed like an angel, pale and beautiful as she wielded a jeweled wand: Zathora's Muse. She waved the Muse over a goblet of red juice and smoke billowed from the cup. A ghostly figure swirled in the smoke, eyes glittering and red lips pursed with satisfaction. "At last," Zathora whispered. Dark-crimson smoke reached out like strangling fingers, pressing against my throat, choking me and—

"Where's that water for Roscoe?"

Frank's voice snapped me back, but even after I gave the dog his water and resumed holding his leash, the vision haunted me.

The vision raised as many questions as it answered. But one thing was clear. Genevieve was not my friend. She was willing to sacrifice me—Jade—to achieve fame.

I could *not* go on stage tonight.

I glanced over at the trash can littered with golden herbs, the natural poison that Genevieve would sprinkle into my juice. There had to be a way to save myself... but I couldn't think of anything.

And hours later, when the world was dark with night, Grey came for me.

23

The night sky was alight with millions of twinkling stars, the air refreshed and washed from hours of rain. A crescent moon lit up the night almost as brightly as a full moon, casting shadows from trees that shifted in the breeze.

Grey held a torch, not a flashlight like normal people, and beamed it in front of us. When I slowed my steps, he nudged me to move faster. I was surprised when we passed the main house and continued down a path I hadn't seen before. Wildflowers and fruit trees bordered the path, but

I couldn't appreciate their beauty. I had a surreal sense of not actually being in my own body, as if I was hovering above and watching the scared girl in the red wig.

Anger flared in me. I would not give in. When it came time to drink the poison, I'd fling it in Genevieve's face and run off the stage. Everyone would be startled, and I could get away before Grey aimed his knife.

I glanced down and saw yellow wildflowers. I shivered, because they reminded me of the deadly brew Genevieve had waiting for me. Then I stumbled to the ground. Grey's bony hands grabbed me right away and lifted me up—but not before I'd snatched a bunch of the yellow flowers and crumpled them into my pocket.

We came to a barn-like structure that was shaded dark green, like the forest, so that it blended in almost invisibly. Lanterns twinkled on each side of the door and moths fluttered near the light. Genevieve would be like a bright light tonight, surprising and delighting an audience who expected little of a woman. I'd sympathized with her, and wanted her to find success. But not like this.

Genevieve was waiting for us. I walked stiffly down a high-ceilinged hallway with her on one side and Grey on the other. We passed vintage posters of famous magicians who stared down at me. A mirror with an ornate frame reflected my fears, and I hardly recognized the red hair, startling red lips, shadowed eyes, and flowing gown that befitted this magician's assistant.

We entered a large theater, and the pounding of my heart merged with an excited buzz of voices. Tiered seats swept down to a stage.

"Thank you, Grey," Genevieve said, giving him a hug. "Wish me luck."

"Of course," he said with a slight bow.

"I'm only the opening act," she said, with a nervous purse of her lips. "You and Josh are the stars tonight. Josh is a sweet boy but I'm rooting for you. You've been such a help to me."

"It's an honor to serve Master Arturo's wife. Go out there and knock them dead."

I flinched at his words.

Genevieve's face glowed as she clasped Grey's hand. "This is it!"

"I'll be watching closely to make sure there are no problems." He turned to me, his twisted lips menacing. "Josh saved me a seat beside him in the front row."

Translation: If you screw up, Josh feels my knife.

The lights in the theater dimmed. With all eyes on us, Genevieve and I made our entrance.

Her jeweled cape flew out behind her as we descended the stairs. As we reached the bottom of the seats and climbed up the four steps to the stage, I got a close look at what awaited me—red candles glowing in a circle around a raised altar, and crystals glittering on a high canopy above.

As I stepped onto an ornamental rug of stars and half-moon symbols, my stomach lurched with dread.

My vision was coming true.

Although I couldn't see Zathora, I sensed her presence. She was hovering invisibly, waiting to make her own entrance. I looked around desperately for an exit, but there was only the main entrance and a side door off the stage—which led either to freedom or to a dressing room. Still, it gave me hope.

Genevieve gestured for me to sit down in a royal-blue velvet chair at the side of the raised altar. I hesitated, unsure whether to keep playing along or make a break for the side door. With an audience of at least fifty men watching my every move, one of them wielding a cache of knives, I didn't argue.

"Welcome lad—I mean, gentlemen," Genevieve announced, projecting her voice so big that she didn't need a microphone. "You all know me as Master Arturo's wife and assistant, but tonight I will startle and surprise you."

A few men nodded, but most sat stoically with amused expressions. These cloaked men were humoring her like she was a cute pet doing tricks. I almost felt sorry for Genevieve, trying so hard to fit in among these chauvinists. But it was hard to sympathize with someone who planned to poison you.

She went on to speak about the history of magicians, citing instances where women proved themselves as competent as men. I shut her out and swept my gaze across the stage. When I saw the goblet and the small gold vial next to it, my breath caught. It wasn't too far away from me, no more than four feet. I knew that the poison wouldn't be added to the juice until the last moment. I reached into my pocket, fingering the crumbling wildflowers. If I could just create a diversion so I could swap the harmless wildflower dust with the golden poison.

Genevieve's voice rose dramatically now as she offered compliments and jokes with the familiarity of long-established friendships. Arturo stood up to praise his wife for her hard work. But he didn't sound very convincing, like he was only humoring her and expected her to bomb.

I spotted Josh and Grey a few seats down. Josh caught my gaze and gestured a thumbs-up. The way his gaze lingered on me was more personal, haunted with regret. But I couldn't think about that now, not when Grey sat beside him, smiling.

Genevieve stepped back, bowing to a polite spatter of applause. I gave another wistful look to the vial on the table, clenching my hand in my pocket.

"Now I'd like to introduce my assistant, the lovely Jade," Genevieve said with a flourish of her hand in my direction.

I knew this was my cue to stand, but my legs were rubber.

"Stage fright," Genevieve said with a musical laugh. "Come on, dear, we mustn't keep the audience waiting."

When I hesitated, I saw Grey glare a warning at me. So I stood and walked toward Genevieve, as we'd practiced, although in rehearsal I only had to walk up to a table, not a sacrificial altar aglow in the flickering candlelight.

"Most stage magic includes mysterious boxes, unbelievable escapes, or shocking disappearances," Genevieve told the audience. "But what I offer you is a story, a journey back centuries ago to an initiation ceremony much like the one we're gathered here for—with one stark difference. Tonight we will witness two worthy apprentices compete for a place in the brotherhood. To win this honor, they will attempt to dazzle us with creative illusions, and one of them will be awarded full membership in the brotherhood."

All gazes swiveled to the front row, where Grey lifted his hand in a confident wave. Josh merely nodded modestly.

"The long-ago society of my story was cloaked in such secrecy that they had very different rules for membership. There was only one way to gain entrance into their society—an initiate had to offer the life of a loved one in trade." She paused, leaning closer, her voice lowered dramatically. "A human sacrifice."

Sharp intakes of breath, including mine, echoed in the

theater. In rehearsal, she'd never shared this speech with me. After my vision of her pact with Zathora, I knew why.

"Imagine an ambitious magician, seeking entry into this legion of magic-keepers," she went on, in such a compelling voice that not even a rustle could be heard from the audience. "But the price he must pay is the sacrifice of his daughter, his only child. Still, his ambition is stronger than his heart, and he lies to his daughter, telling her he's taking her on a special trip. And he dresses her in a gown of fine silk and rows her on a boat to a private island. She's excited, trusting, but when she sees the tears in her father's eyes, she becomes scared and tries to run back to the boat. But her father holds her firmly and leads her into a cave where candles are lit and crystals shine with earth energy. And he forces her to an altar … just like this one."

This was my cue to walk to the altar, to stand there as if in a trance and wait for Genevieve to hand me the goblet. I took one step forward … then froze.

Movement flickered above me—a wisp of something spectral with shining eyes.

Zathora has arrived, I thought bitterly.

"The young girl is frightened, staring around at masked figures and too terrified to move," Genevieve improvised. "But she trusts her father and steps up to the altar."

Still, I didn't move.

"She steps up to the altar," Genevieve repeated, giving

me a look. But it wasn't her look that made me move; it was Grey's quick flash of a knife and his nod toward Josh.

"The father's shoulders heaved and he cried out, 'No! I've changed my mind. I'm taking her home where she's safe.' But the Master Magician snapped his fingers and four cloaked men pulled the father away. Then the Master Magician threw off her cloak, revealing a woman with pale hair and unimaginable skills. She spoke gently to the girl, assuring her she was safe and among friends. The Master Magician offered the girl a drink to calm her nerves."

Genevieve reached for the goblet, lifting it with drama. I watched with horror as she subtly grasped the glass vial with her other hand and twisted the lid. Then she set the goblet down, lifting her empty hand with a dramatic gesture. While all eyes were on that hand, she slipped her other hand behind her back, positioning it directly over the goblet. No one other than me—and Zathora—saw her dump the poison into the drink.

Genevieve held out the cup to me.

"And the young girl trusted the Master Magician, and took the goblet and drank—unaware that it was deadly poison and she was the sacrifice."

I took the cup ... but I didn't drink.

"Jade," Genevieve said through clenched teeth, "drink!"

I shook my head. "Don't do this."

"We rehearsed this a hundred times."

"But not with real poison."

"Don't be silly. It's all an illusion. You'll be fine."

But would Josh? I stole a glance at Grey, catching a flash of the knife in his hand.

"Come on, Jade," she wheedled in a softer tone. "Everyone is waiting."

"No!" I shoved the goblet at her, and as it started to fall she made a grab for it so that only one blood-red drop fell to the floor. "I know about Zathora."

She clutched the goblet to her chest. "How … How could you know?"

"I saw her and heard you talking."

"Impossible! No one can see her but me!"

The audience was buzzed with whispers and chuckles as if they'd expected a farce from a woman magician. I hated them for mocking her, yet I hated her for using me.

"I can see Zathora. She's over there." I pointed toward the altar where a filmy shape merged into the smoky trails from candles. She was easier to see now, fury darkening her aura. I could feel her energy building like a storm. "She's wearing the costume she died in and she's stronger than most ghosts I've met."

"You've met other ghosts?" Still clutching the goblet to her chest, Genevieve staggered back with shock. "But … but how?"

I glanced at the audience, full of magicians who had vowed to debunk psychics and believed that ghosts did not exist. My words hadn't been spoken loudly, yet I knew they'd been heard. The chuckles faded to an angry silence.

"Jade couldn't see ghosts, but I can." I'd gone too far, but I was too angry and scared to stop now. I whipped off the red wig and tossed it on the ground like something dead. "I'm her sister Sabine—and I'm psychic."

With a whoosh of cold air, Zathora soared toward me, the glittering Muse in her hand like an avenging sword. "Foolish girl!" the ghost shrieked, no longer a shadowy fog but as solid and as real as a living person. From the cries in the audience, I knew others saw her, too.

"Stay away from me!" I cried, backing up.

"Kill her now and be done with this nonsense!" Zathora hissed.

Genevieve looked in bewilderment from me to the ghost, so pale she could be a ghost herself. Her gaze swiveled to the men in the audience—some were pointing but most were sitting still in their seats, shocked. Zathora's rage made her visible to everyone.

"You're ruining everything!" Genevieve wailed. "This was supposed to be my night and now they're all laughing at me."

"You shouldn't have lied to me!" I retorted. "You can't make me drink poison!"

"The show must go on, and if you won't do it, then I will." Genevieve's gaze was focused on the goblet and her next words were so low I almost didn't hear them. "Zathora will tell you how to bring me back—after I'm dead."

Then Genevieve put the goblet to her lips.

And fell to the floor.

Dead.

24

Shouts rang from the audience, and the first to reach the stage was Arturo.

Sobbing, he cradled his wife in his arms. "Gen, oh why … why?"

"She wanted respect," I said softly.

"I respect her. I love her. There isn't anything I wouldn't do for her." The balding man looked up, tears streaking down his cheeks. "I don't know what to do … she's not breathing. Oh my god! Please, if you know how to help her ... do it!"

Darkly garbed magicians were rising from their chairs, coming to the stage. I could escape now, and no one would stop me in the pandemonium. But Genevieve looked so helpless, so broken. And I remembered her last words.

"Arturo, I can help!" I said quickly, fear rising as I noticed Grey coming toward the stage. "I can find out how to bring her back, but not if the others crowd the stage."

Arturo didn't hesitate, waving his arms high and whistling for quiet. He ordered them to return to their seats. He spoke powerfully, with tears still falling from his eyes. The audience obeyed. Even Grey backed up, his hands concealed under his cloak.

"Do whatever you can," Arturo said, turning back to me.

"Even if it involves a ghost?"

"There's no such ... oh, damn it. I know what I saw. Just save her!" His reply showed that if he had to choose between his wife and success, he chose his wife.

"Zathora," I called out, shivering in the ghost-cold air. She'd faded, but her wand still glittered brightly so I knew she was there. "Can you hear me?"

The air whirled with flickering shadows, one shape solidifying in the air mere feet above me. "I care not to hear from you."

"This is your fault," I accused her. "Tell me how to revive Genevieve."

Her dark eyes flashed. "Why should I?"

"Because you owe it to her."

"I owe no one," she said haughtily.

"She's dying because of you!"

"I beg to differ. She's already dead."

Her tone was sharp and petulant, so distant from compassion that I knew appealing to her conscience would never work. I tried a different tactic.

"If you let her die, you'll never get another chance to reclaim your reputation. Look around—this audience is full of magicians who didn't believe ghosts exist, but they see you now. They can't deny the truth. Revive Genevieve and you will be respected as a master magician."

Her form darkened, but I could tell I had her interest. I continued. "Don't you want to be famous as the only magician to bring the dead back to life?"

"I am the only one with that knowledge," she boasted. "But I won't help you, not after you spoiled everything."

"I didn't take the drink, but Genevieve did. If you bring her back, you will have proved you can achieve miracles. You'll be famous!"

"Famous isn't enough!" Zathora snapped. "Foolish girl, do you not realize that my goal is not fame? I wanted you!"

"Me?" I stumbled back a step.

"Your lovely, youthful body. Once your soul had left, I planned to slip in and bring myself back to life as I meant to a century ago. In your body, I would have a long life ahead as the most powerful magician in this world. The secrets I can bring to the magician world are astounding."

"So you really *were* going to kill me?" I demanded. "Did Genevieve know?"

"Don't be foolish! Of course not, or she never would have helped me. She thought you would be safe. But now it's all for nothing. I refuse to begin again as a middle-aged woman. Let her die."

"No! Bring her back!" I begged.

"I see nothing in it for me." Zathora floated higher, her essence moving the crystals so chimes sang with her laughter.

I wasn't sure how much Arturo could hear or see, but he seemed to know that his wife was slipping away with the ghost. He clutched my gown. "Do something! Please!"

What could I do? I had no power over a ghost.

But I do, a voice spoke in my head.

"Opal!" I cried, ignoring the puzzled look from Arturo.

I have told you I am never far away, I merely allow you to discover your own path. But I won't allow another spirit to interfere with my duty toward you.

"So you'll help?"

As you might say, it's time to kick some ghost butt.

"So let's kick it," I told her.

"What is that disturbance?" Zathora called out, wavering closer to me. The jewels on the Muse glowed brighter, as if it were solid enough for me to reach out and grab it.

Do it! Take it! Opal urged.

"Take what?"

Do you remember the message I passed on to you?

I started to say no, but then it came back to me: *Hold close the crystal staff to save heart or the old soul seeking to command death will steal beyond life.*

The old soul was Zathora, and the crystal staff had to be the Muse.

So I jumped into the air and grabbed hold of Zathora's Muse. I wasn't sure who was more surprised when the wand slipped from her hand to mine. And it was real, solid, and blazing with power. As Zathora reached out for me, a wave of cold air swept her like she was caught up in a tidal wave. A tidal wave named Opal. Go, Opal!

"Help my wife," Arturo pleaded.

I looked at the wand, unsure for a moment, and then I just knew what to do. I held the Muse purposefully and visualized Genevieve, radiant and alive. I pushed aside my anger toward her and remembered her laughter and kindnesses. She'd never meant to hurt me, after all, but had been tricked by the lies of a twisted ghost.

Lightness flowed around me as I embraced all the loving, wonderful things about life. Very carefully I brought the tip of the wand down to Genevieve and touched her heart. *Save heart.*

Electricity surged through me, as if lightning was mixing with fireworks. Pushed backwards, the world spun for a moment, then slowed. Stars burst around me and I came close to fainting for real. But then I heard a sound that shocked me back to awareness. A moan... from Genevieve.

"Gen!" Arturo cried joyfully, as his wife's eyes flickered open. "You're alive."

She lifted her head, smiling. "Did you ever doubt me?"

Sobbing, he buried his face in her blond hair and embraced his wife. The audience sprang to life, chairs scraping and men shouting.

This was my cue to get the hell out of there. I tucked Zathora's wand in my back pocket and hurried to the door at the side of the stage, which in fact opened to the outside. The night had calmed—no breeze, only sparkling stars and a moon sliced into a curving smile.

I'd only taken a few steps when a voice called, "Wait! Sabine."

I turned to see Josh hurrying toward me, looking a little like Harry Potter with his black cloak flapping behind him.

"Where are you going?" he asked, bending slightly to catch his breath.

"Far away from here. I've had enough."

"I know ... I mean, what happened on the stage ... it was ... unbelievable!" He started to reach for me but stiffened. "Are you all right? Were you hurt by that ... well, whatever it was?"

"I'm fine. But I'll be better when I'm at home where I belong. Sorry I won't see your performance."

"As if that's going to happen—definitely not tonight. Everyone's too freaked out."

"Yeah, I kind of figured."

Josh rubbed his forehead, frowning. "When Genevieve started breathing again, Grey acted really strange. Instead of going to see how she was doing, he took off."

"He ran away because he knew that Genevieve would tell the brotherhood how they'd conspired with a ghost. Grey pretended not to believe in ghosts, but he supported Genevieve's plan to bring one back from the dead in exchange for influence with her husband. Grey was determined to win the competition at all costs."

"You don't have any proof of that," Josh argued.

"I heard him. He threatened me and Jade, and like I told you, he even threatened you—he said he'd kill you if Jade tried to leave."

"I just can't believe that. He's my friend ..." Josh sounded a little less sure this time.

"He's *not* a good guy, Josh, but you are," I said softly. "Did you know that's why Jade came here? She wanted to rescue you."

"Why?" He blinked. "We hardly know each other."

"She couldn't figure it out either."

"I never even saw her while she was here. I wish I could thank her."

"She's dating Evan, so you can thank her when you get home."

"I will." He shifted uneasily. "But I wonder about ... well, what now?"

"I'm out of here—even if I have to hike for miles in the dark."

"You won't have to do that. I'll give you a flashlight."

"Modern technology in this place?"

"Hey, it gets dark at night. You should see what the other guys have stashed—video games, iPods, cameras, and one dude even has a mini battery-operated refrigerator stocked with energy drinks. The old guys like Arturo and Henry are strict about rules, but the rest of us enjoy our secrets."

"You don't have to stay here," I told him. "Come with me."

Josh shook his head. "Tonight was weird, but these guys are my friends and I want to learn from them. I'll stay until the initiation ceremony so I can do my performance. Then, whether I'm chosen or not, I'll be home for Christmas like I promised my parents."

"They'll be glad to see you."

"Not only them."

I tensed, afraid of what he might say.

"Horse, too," he added, which made us both smile.

I touched his hand softly. "Josh, I really am sorry ... for everything."

"After what I think I saw tonight, I owe you an apology ... things I was so sure about, well, I'm going to have to think about them."

"I understand."

"Do you think we ... I mean ... we could ...?"

I put my hand to his lips. "Don't say it. Let's just ..."

"Be friends?" He groaned. "Please don't say that."

"I won't. I respect you too much."

He sighed, looking deep into my eyes. My heart stirred for a moment, until an image of Dominic came to me. Josh was a great guy ... just not my guy.

I wasn't sure what to say, knowing we'd see each other at school and not wanting to lose him as a good friend. So I stepped back and simply asked, "Are we okay?"

"Sure." He gave me a wry smile. "We're cool."

"But that isn't." I pointed to the small inked PFC on his arm. Performers against Frauds and Charlatans. "That tatt has to go."

"Why? Doesn't it make me look dangerous?"

I laughed. "Not even."

"What if I change the meaning?"

"Performers For Clairvoyants?" I joked.

"Don't push your luck," he teased. "I'm not sure what I saw or believe. It could have been an elaborate trick."

"Ghosts are real and you know it now, even if you're afraid to admit it."

"I'm not afraid... just confused. But I can't deny I saw something... a ghost?" He looked at me for confirmation and I nodded. "So ghosts are real?"

"Not just ghosts." I pointed to myself. "Psychics, too."

*   *   *

Having a flashlight made hiking along the trail much easier, but it was scary being alone in the woods at night. Every time I heard a sound, I jumped nervously and shone my flashlight around. I never saw anything... but I was sure the night creatures saw me.

When I neared the dam, so close to freedom, I started to relax—until I saw the lights.

Two bobbing orbs, floating like ghosts, came down the path toward me. I was too exhausted to deal with any more ghosts tonight. Just go away, I thought. But the lights grew brighter, and then were so close I could see the shapes behind the orbs.

A voice shattered the night. "Stop right there, whoever you are!"

And I started laughing, crying, and running all at the same time.

"Dad!" I cried, throwing my arms around him. "Oh my god! I never expected to see you here!"

"Sabine! It really is you!" Dad squeezed me tight and whirled me off the ground like I was still a little girl.

"How did you get here?" I asked him. "And who's with you?"

The other figure stepped out of a shadow, her black hair making her blend in with the night except for the streak of pink in it and her pale face makeup. "You sure cause a lot of trouble," Thorn griped.

"I've been told that before," I said, giggling.

"We came to rescue you, but it looks like you rescued yourself."

"I'll tell you everything once we're out of here. How did you find me?"

"Duh," Thorn said. "I'm a Finder."

"But Jade helped too." Dad held me tight, ruffling my hair fondly. "We would have come sooner, but I only found out where you were a few hours ago. Jade called from Reno."

"Reno!" I started to ask what she was doing there, but then guessed she'd gone after her mother. Poor Jade. My mother might be bossy and annoying a lot, but at least she acted like a mother.

On the way to the car, Dad explained that Nona called him, frantic because I was missing. They'd called my friends, and Manny told them I'd texted him about going to Arturo's property. Thorn told Dad she had a feeling I was near a lake and offered to come along to help find me. But when they drove up here, they didn't see my car and couldn't get past Arturo's security guards.

They were ready to go to the police when Dad's cell phone rang. It was Jade. After apologizing for not calling sooner, she told them how to get through the fence and follow the path by the dam.

Then I was inside Dad's car, inhaling the sweet lemon scent of the hanging air freshener. It was my turn for explanations, but suddenly I was so tired. One moment I was talking to Thorn, and the next I was waking up as the car pulled in at Nona's house. Dad half-carried me into the house, which felt so safe.

Thorn agreed to stay the night since it was so late, and Nona found a fold-out bed that Dad carried to my attic room. I sorted through my nightlight collection and chose a butterfly, not because it had any deep meaning, but because it had been a gift from Dad. Tonight he'd really come through for me.

Thorn borrowed pajamas from me, then crawled underneath the covers.

I tugged my covers over me, too hyped now to relax. My short nap had revived me and I wasn't ready to go to sleep quite yet.

"Thorn, now that we're alone, I want to hear everything."

She turned toward me, propped on one elbow and looking about twelve without her makeup. "About what?" she asked, yawning.

"You know," I said impatiently. "Jacques? His murder? And what about that folder you saw in Jacques' apartment?"

"Oh, Pen and I found out a lot." A slow smile played on Thorn's face." I know who killed Jacques."

25

Since she wasn't a big talker, Thorn's explanation was like a text—lots of details were missing. Still, I was able to get most of the story.

While Penny-Love had been ready to forget about the whole "Jacques" drama, Thorn couldn't stop thinking about it—especially that folder. "It seemed like such a coincidence to find photos of Josh and Grey in Jacques' apartment," she said. "I even dreamed about that folder. I had to find it. So I Googled everything I could about Oscar-aka-Jacques.

From the memorial announcement, I found out names and addresses of his family, partner, and other police officers. Also, thanks to Manny's hacking skills, I learned that a suspect was being sought for questioning in the murder."

She went on to describe the "suspect," a guy in his twenties with a snake tattoo coiled on his cheek. Hoping to find the folder, Thorn drove to Jacque's partner's house and parked across the street. Just after she arrived, a car pulled up and parked in the driveway—driven by none other than Snake Tattoo.

Thorn spied through her window and used her phone to snap pictures as Jacques' partner—the guy with the sideburns they'd followed to the memorial service—came outside to meet Snake Tattoo. Once the men went inside, Thorn's Finding radar led her to Sideburn's car, which was fortunately unlocked. She found the boxes from Jacques' apartment—and the folder. She took the folder home, and using an account Manny assured her was untraceable, emailed her photos of the meeting between Sideburns and Snake Tattoo to the detective in charge of Jacque's murder.

When she read through the folder, she discovered that it wasn't a coincidence that Jacques had information on Josh and Grey. Jacques suspected Grey of several crimes, including the vandalism at Trick or Treats, and according to his notes, he thought Josh's disappearance was suspicious. Since he was already working undercover at Sheridan High, he'd started to check into Grey's background.

There were notes in the folder on Grey's disturbing history of violence—he'd attacked a girlfriend after she'd gone to a psychic who had warned her to stop dating him, and he'd been arrested for torching a New Age shop and nearly killing the owner. He'd jumped bail, and there was still an outstanding warrant for Thomas Greyson—which turned out to be only one of Grey's aliases.

I shivered, realizing how close I'd come to finding out just how violent Grey could be.

"You won't believe what happened next," Thorn said dramatically. Then she described how she drove back to Sideburns' house but parked a distance away. From the safety of her car, she heard sirens and saw flashing lights surround the house. Cops stormed inside and within minutes, it was over. Snake Tattoo was led out in handcuffs—and so was Jacques' partner, his head down in surrender.

"Later, I found out from Manny that Jacque's partner, Richard something, confessed to taking bribes from Snake Tattoo, who is a drug dealer. Richard had encouraged Jacques to keep investigating Grey because it kept him busy and out of the way. But this backfired. When Jacques found out that Grey had an outstanding warrant, he told Richard to come to his apartment because he'd discovered something important. Snake Tattoo heard about this and assumed Jacques knew about the bribes. It was Snake Tattoo who killed Jacques."

"What about the folder?" I asked Thorn. "Did you return it?"

"Sure. I drove to a police station and left it there anonymously. Also the gun that Cheerleader stupidly took."

"I hope you wiped off the fingerprints so they can't trace you."

"Do I look stupid?" she demanded. "Me, you, and Cheerleader are safe. But not Grey. I got a text a while ago from Manny saying that Grey is now a guest of the judicial system. I was wondering when they'd catch him."

"You sound like you knew they would."

She nodded. "Well, yeah. Before I turned in the folder, I tried my Finding on the photo of Grey, then I made an anonymous phone call to the police with an address. That dude won't threaten my friends again."

"Wow," was all I could say. "You were like a real detective. You could have a great career in law enforcement."

"That's not what you predicted in the Mystic Manny column. You said I'd travel, make friends, and find interesting experiences—very generic fortune-telling."

"I'm not really great with predictions," I admitted. "Manny pushed me to come up with those fast."

"Manny can be a pain in the ass," Thorn said, smiling. "But he's cool, and a real friend. I sent him a text so he'd know you were okay."

"He was worried?" I asked, surprised.

"Not just him. Manny and Pen stayed with Nona while I went with your dad. Finding you was the best moment ever."

"For me too. Thanks so much. You are ... well ... a real friend," I said with a catch in my throat. I knew Thorn hated emotional displays. Still, I wanted to do something for her. So I crossed my room, opened a drawer, and grasped a long slim object.

When I held out my hand to Thorn, she arched her pierced brow. "What's that?"

"Zathora's wand. The real one, not the fake."

"So it's valuable?"

"Probably ... but completely unexplainable. I don't want it. Do you?"

"An evil magic wand? Cool. Does it do magic tricks?"

"Not anymore," I said. I was sure this was true. While walking in the woods, I'd tried using it to bring up an image of Dominic and gotten nothing. I glanced down at my hands, clasped together, and hesitated before asking the question in my heart. "Has there been any news about Dominic?"

"Sorry." Thorn shook her head. "Nothing."

The worst fears echoed in my mind: I'd never see Dominic again.

Thorn scooted next to me and squeezed my hand. "I can try Finding him for you."

It was tempting, but I shook my head. "He'll come back when he's ready ... if he can."

"Don't stress, he'll be okay. He's too crazy about you to stay away long. I'll bet he shows up for Christmas."

I wished so hard for that, it was like there was a wishing muscle in my body that strained and pulled, aching from the effort. But I had to face facts. Dominic couldn't come home if he was in jail.

Yawning, I turned away from Thorn and closed my eyes.

When I awoke the next morning, she was already gone.

Walking downstairs, I stared at the glittering colored lights of our Christmas tree. Pine scented the living room and tiny glass angels decorated a shelf above the couch. I wanted to feel excited about the holiday, but my heart was too empty. I wondered if Dominic would ever open the gift wrapped for him—a falconer's glove engraved with *DS*. I'd had it done a few weeks ago, before I knew his real last name. Not that it mattered now...not without Dominic.

Nona was so happy to have me home that I tried to get into the holiday spirit for her. As we baked sugar cookies shaped like stars, trees, and snowmen, Nona had news of her own to share. Apparently the glow had tarnished on the Heart Lights merger. When Roger started bossing Nona around and telling her how to run her business, she'd shown him the door. I was relieved. No one could run Soul-Mate Matches better than Nona.

The house filled with delicious baking scents and the day passed quickly. I texted and emailed friends, reassuring everyone I was back to normal—and trying to convince myself, too.

Tomorrow was Christmas Eve, and Nona had invited some friends over. Most of my friends had plans with their own families, so it would be a small party of four: Nona's card-playing pal Grady, Velvet, Nona, and myself. On Christmas morning, Nona and I would join my parents for a festive celebration at their house. My mother had even (shock!) invited Jade. I'd found this out from Jade herself—she'd called to apologize for getting caught up in her mother's drama and not contacting our dad right away. She hesitated, then told me about the invite.

"Are you okay with me sharing in your family celebration?" she asked, sounding oddly vulnerable.

"It's more than okay. Dad will be thrilled to have all of his daughters there." Then I added with a laugh, "But my family gets kind of intense. Just warning you."

There were last minute gifts to buy, so on Christmas Eve I headed to the mall with Penny-Love. She helped keep my mind off Dominic by sharing gossip and confiding about the new guy she'd met—a year younger than her but seriously hot. She was sure he'd ask her to the New Year's Dance, but if he was too shy, she'd ask him.

By the time she dropped me off, it was dark.

Carrying shopping bags, I went inside, prepared to turn on holiday music and wrap gifts till Grady and Velvet showed up.

Sprawling on my bedroom floor, I unrolled foil wrapping paper and snipped off a large piece with scissors. As I reached for it, a blur of calico fur pounced on the paper.

"Lilybelle!" I cried. "You bad cat!"

She swished her tail and sat down right on the ripped wrapping paper, staring up at me.

"Shoo!" I waved her away. "Can't you see I'm busy?"

She meowed haughtily, then got up and strode to my door. She meowed, the way she did when her food or water bowl was empty. But her stare was different, giving me chills. She'd only acted this strange one other time.

Jumping up, I tossed the scissors aside and followed her out of the room. I only slowed to grab a jacket, then my cat and I were out the door, racing down the steps and heading for the woods.

As I ran, I warned myself that I could be wrong. He might not be there, which would be disappointing.

But Christmas Eve was a time for miracles.

And when I reached the tree house, I looked up—and saw the guy I loved.

"Dominic!" I sobbed, lifting my arms up for him.

His strong fingers curled around my wrists and he gently pulled me into the tree house. Dagger perched on the window ledge, watching.

"Sabine," Dominic said, my name sounding so amazing on his lips. His arms circled my waist and he led me to the couch. "You have no idea how good it feels to hold you again."

"Oh, I have a really good idea."

"It's like we're been apart for years."

"Longer. And I've been so worried."

"I'm sorry, but things were crazy." He gently brushed a loose strand of hair from my face. "During everything, I kept thinking of this moment. How great it would be to see you again … and how I was going to do this."

He pulled me close and softly pressed his lips against mine. I heard a flutter of wings and the scurry of tiny animals around us, yet it was if we were completely alone in our own tree-top world. I leaned into him and closed my eyes, lost in wonderful emotions.

"God, you're so beautiful," he whispered, pulling back to stare at me as if he was seeing me for the first time.

I captured his hand in mind, squeezing tight. "You're not getting away from me again. This is where you belong. No arguments."

"Does it look like I'm arguing? Home is on the farm with you and Nona."

Relief swept through me as I looked into his wonderful face. "I've missed you so much."

"Me too. Only more."

I shifted on the couch. "Then why didn't you call?"

"I couldn't. My lawyer wouldn't allow me to contact anyone."

"Lawyer?" Fears knotted in my stomach. "So you were arrested?"

"No, but it's been a legal mess because I've been living under a fake name, and there were tons of papers to sign. The PI flew me to New Jersey, where I met the lawyer who is handling my uncle's estate."

"What? I don't understand."

"Neither did I, at first. I kept expecting red flashing lights and cops. The PI wouldn't tell me anything until we met with the lawyer. I wanted to call you a million times, but I couldn't until I was sure about what happened to my uncle."

"And are you sure now?"

He nodded, stroking my hair. "I'm sure—about a lot of things."

I smiled up at him, holding tighter, not ever wanting to let go.

"So what happened to your uncle?" I asked. "He's dead, isn't he?"

"Very. But I didn't do it." A huge grin spread across his face. "It was natural causes."

"What a relief!"

"Yeah ... it's like I'm finally free," he admitted. "My uncle died only a year ago. He'd inherited money and a house on Long Island from a great aunt. While I spent all those years thinking I'd killed him, he was sunning on the beach. Then he had a heart attack and didn't leave a will, so his lawyers hired the PI to find me."

"So he wasn't lying when he said you had inherited money!" I exclaimed.

"There's enough for college, to start my own business, and to take you out to a really expensive restaurant." He grinned wickedly. "Or we could just stay here."

"I'd like that," I whispered, warm desire spreading through me. "But Nona is having a party... it's Christmas Eve."

"Yes, I know. But I haven't had a chance to buy you anything."

"You're here. Best Christmas gift ever."

"I'm going to be here for a long time," he told me.

I thought of Nona waiting for me. "We should go to the house."

"Yeah, we should." Dominic's hand traced my cheek and my lips, then slipped away as he stood up. "Bookmark our place."

"Until later," I said softly.

Dominic nodded. "We'll have lots of time together now that I'm not a wanted man anymore."

"You're wanted... by me."

He chuckled. "So isn't it time we did something normal? Like go out on a date? Movie, dinner, dancing, horseback riding or something."

"Or something," I said, leaning into him. "Just being with you is all I want."

"You've got me."

"And I'm never letting go." I brushed my lips across his. "This feels so right. I can't wait to see what's next."

"Don't you already know?" he asked lightly. "Since you're psychic?"

"I hardly ever know important stuff about myself and the people I love," I murmured. I reached out, entwining my fingers in his. "Sometimes it's better to just enjoy the surprises along the way. Together."

"We'll be together for a very long time," Dominic said softly.

"Is that a prediction?" I teased.

"A promise."

Holding hands, I looked deep into his eyes and glimpsed our future.

I couldn't wait.

The End

MYSTIC MANNY'S
TWELVE
10-YEARS-IN-THE-FUTURE
PREDICTIONS

Penny-Love—Reality show star after giving birth to her own clone.

Kaitlyn—After jilting her fiancé at the altar, she joins the Army.

Catelyn—Keeping up with her BFF Kaitlyn, she joins the Army, too.

Mr. Blankenship—The teacher with bad taste in ties gets rich selling tacky ties on the Home Shopping Network.

Yvette—The school newspaper photographer has a successful business taking pictures of celebrity pets.

K.C.—Not being noticed comes in handy! Works in Reno at a mall as a store detective. Shoplifters beware!

Thorn—Travels, makes new friends, and finds interesting experiences.

Josh—Pediatrician by day and at night stars in a magic show with the hottest new female magician in town.

Evan—Goes into politics.

Zach—Drops out of school. Homeless. Organizing a street union.

Jill—Mother of three, CEO, and volunteer at women's shelter.

Manny—The writer of these predictions remains totally awesome.

DRAMA PRESENT
Mary Shelley's
FRANKENSTEI

By Connie Goldsmith

At night, the grounds of our sc relatively deserted. However, l urday the lights shone bright the Little Theatre, calling vi to see the drama departmen *kenstein*, in which a brilliar scientist battles the lonely cr made from pieces of the de Shelley was twenty years her novel *Frankenstein* was anonymously in 1818.

"The students—both cast a have really worked hard on said Erin Dealey, whose sn department is funded in par performances. "I'm so prou Pulling off a huge producti takes teamwork and dedi they've really gotten into it.

Molly Blaisdell, a senio cast in a non-traditional the troubled Victor Frank agrees to create a bride for and unwittingly plunges h into murder, despair, and

Andrew Davidson, a plays the creature, wh geance against Franke the scientist destroys t

CPSIA information can be obtained at www.ICGtesting.com
Printed in the USA
BVOW08s2338151013

333822BV00003B/30/P

9 780738 719573